# And The Hound Of Asgard

## By

## David A. Burt

Cover design: Scott Gaunt.
Troll illustration by Anna Wolkowicka

Many thanks to Mum, Dad and Leanne for encouragement, to Anna for her love of fantasy, to Greg, Madeline and Zara for invaluable advice, to Suzy for championing the screenplay, to Steve for good sense and Alex for liking the trolls. Many thanks in particular to Isla and Heather for motivation and for their insights into Norse mythology and dogs in particular.

# Preface

My story is based in London and Oslo. I'm from North Yorkshire but know London well, and was fortunate enough to go to school in Oslo for a couple of years.

Like many expat families we had a resident troll, a 2ft tall wax grotesque we named after the landlord, and at school I was probably more exposed to the folklore of Norse mythology than the average British kid.

In 2008 I decided to start writing a script, set in Norway, which would have trolls, Thor, and a dog in it. Ideally the dog would be of the talking, somewhat demonically possessed variety. I thought a small indignant dog would be good, possibly a mongrel with some Yorkshire Terrier in the mix.

Thor would be somewhat practical, a little older and grounded in the real world. I remembered that the Norse gods had the power to change appearance and thought it would be interesting if the war-like, bearded, Thor was to become Thora, particularly should a gent be unwise enough to approach her.

I also learnt that Thora translates to Thunder Goddess, so this seemed to be the right choice.

In terms of other characters, the hero, Terry, came from the four Terrys of British comedy; Pratchett, Chapman, Jones and Scott.

Ketil was named after a Norwegian friend whilst Anders (Andy) and Clive helped by reading an early version of the script.

Inger from Knogsvinger was an utter fabrication, and I do hope that should any Ingers from Kongsvinger be in the scarf business that they appreciate that this is an entirely unintentional coincidence.

As far as Snorri Snakker goes, Snorri was the author of The Prose Edda and Snakker is Norwegian for speaking. This is something I remember from learning the phrase, 'I don't speak Norwegian, I speak English'. As a blue eyed, fair haired boy in Norway, this was something I said most days.

Whereas its normal to write a book first and then adapt it to a script, I have done it the other way around. Ultimately, scripts are written to be read, or ideally made, and I thought it was time to get it out there. I do hope you enjoy the book.

-----

'Look what I'm dealing with man, I'm dealing with fools and trolls'

Charlie Sheen

Given sufficient uplift a raven can go quite far without flapping, whether in terms of vertical flapping, elliptical flapping or just in terms of being agitated and a bit panicky. Today, Hugin was gliding, bouncing on the thermals as it were, and he was in his element.

Mountainous land flew by beneath him, the landscape passing from rolling green to cliffs and then the sea. He tipped a wing and barrel rolled, diving fast and then levelling to skim the waves. Hugin was an envoy and rather serious in appearance. He was also a hedonist, albeit one without much time for fun, and enjoyed pulling aerials when no one was looking.

He spotted a boat and climbed to a more appropriate altitude, proceeding with dignity, the very epitome of a graven raven. As expected, the boat contained two persons; Thor, a simply dressed Viking in his 50s, and Hymir, a giant of indeterminate age wearing a light brown jerkin.

As Hugin glided towards them he took in their dynamic. Hymir was perched rather incongruously on one end, whilst Thor, far the shorter of the two, was rowing.

Whereas they were both perfectly strong enough to row a boat, it was unlikely that Hymir would get a turn.

Thor's ego, once satiated by war, had ebbed into the braggadocio of a competitive fisherman. Hymir didn't like fishing to start with, and the two of them didn't fit well on a small dory.

Hugin slowed his approach with a minor tilt, landed on the boat's rail and regarded the men. He bowed and cleared his throat to speak but was interrupted.

"Sod off," said Hymir.

Hugin flapped and not in a good way. Startled he lost his footing and slipped off the side of the boat. Without space to recover himself he landed with a splash. Hugin surmised that they were best left to resume their business and had no message in urgent need of dispatch. He climbed damply to altitude, with the giant's growl close behind him.

Thor watched him with amusement, leaning forward on his oars, "You always did have a way with nature."

"I prefer my nature between two thick loaves of Vollkornbrod."

"Even small birds?"

"One eats what one can. Even little ravens such as Hugin. Their small bones make excellent toothpicks."

"You're far too big for small ravens," said Thor, upping the bravado. "I'll row to deeper waters for bigger sport. Let's find a beast that will match your girth."

Hymir looked a little reluctant. "There's plenty of fish round here. If we're lucky we'll catch a whale."

"Still too small." Thor pulled up his sleeves. "Not entirely keen on deep water fishing, are you? Matters not. Out to the ocean we go." He grabbed the oars and heaved to.

The boat sped off under his phenomenal strength. "There. Now we'll have some fun. Where's the bait?" Thor opened a box lid to find a large Ox's head. He lifted the head into the sky, examining it.

"My prize oxen!" Hymir exclaimed.

Thor smiled and attached the bait to a large hook and line. "Not anymore. Here fishy fishy."

Bearing in mind Thor had decapitated his ox and was very much intent on deep sea fishing, there was little Hymir could do by way of recourse, at least of practical use. He felt like smashing up the boat but couldn't swim. Thor had the awful egocentric gleam in his eyes of a psycho consumed with a mission. Hymir resolved not to agree to fishing with him again.

Thor cast his line and the head went flying, landing with a splash in the ocean, where it bobbed for a moment then sank. "I've cast the bait. Let's see what Njörðr brings us for dinner."

The sun went down and it was a moonlit night with a brilliant array of stars. Hymir was asleep holding a lantern against his chest. The line tugged and Thor stirred. "Wake up old man," he said. "We've got a nibble."

Hymir woke with a start and looked around anxiously. "I was only pretending to be asleep. What is it?"

"Whatever it is, it's got a taste for ox head. Perhaps I should have used ox tail. We could have made soup."

Something was approaching the rapidly slackening line. Thor reeled in swiftly as a shape raced towards them, just beneath the surface. The line suddenly started reeling out as the shape disappeared, diving deep. "Oh no you don't." He gave an almighty heave and his foot crashed through the bottom of the boat. "You devil."

The creature surfaced right in front of them, it was a serpent, light grey in colour, like a wet dragon without wings. It thrashed and tried to break free.

"Release it!" Hymir shouted. The serpent thrashed further dragging the boat with it. Hymir scrambled for his knife. "It'll destroy us. Release it I say!"

"Where's my hammer?" Thor grasped for his hammer, raised it and went face to face with the serpent. "Midgard Serpent. Meet Mjolnir. At last."

A hissing voice came from the serpent, venom dripping from its words. "Now is not the time. Assssguardian."

Thor raised his hammer and lightning sparked the sky. Hymir cut the line and the Midgard Serpent darted backwards, the hammer looked like it was going to miss... Thor roared.

Darkness.


A beat-up Lada cabriolet, top down, raced through a long tunnel, down the E16 highway towards Oslo. In the back seat was a Yorkshire Terrier, fur blown back on his face.

Next to the dog sat Haakon Lingard, an earnest man in the autumn of his 30s, sporting a Mexican moustache and smooth Scandinavian knitwear. In the passenger seat, Imre Tyll, a 40 something Hungarian - an archetypal hipster in skinny jeans, with his beard twitching in the passing air.

Reading the road with steely determination was Terry Chadwick, 40, in a cardigan he knitted himself. A stoic man with a hint of burnt out heroism, Terry would emerge from most disasters, blinking and staggering but alive.

Terry and his friends were on the way back from a knitwear event in Bergen. Terry once dreamt of rolling a giant ball of wool from the expo all the way through the foyer to the carpark and lighting the thread like a fuse. In his dream the whole place would go up like a knitted schematic of an explosion, with yarn shooting into the sky like rockets.

It's fair to say the expo had not been a success. Terry didn't like competitors and the expo had been full of them, often selling better stock. He sometimes bought more than he sold. In truth, he was glad to see the back of it and of the woman who had enticed him into this world, Inger.

Terry's life to date had been a litany of mismanagement and poor choices at key junctures. It was the usual story; man meets a girl, falls in love, she's got a loom, and before you know it you've bought into the cardigan business. But weaving didn't always pay, and then things started unravelling.

He'd taken his eye off the ball and ended up divorced and with a significant investment he couldn't shift. As Terry was fond of saying, usually in bars to strangers, "Inger. What could go wrong with a girl called Inger? Turns out it's short for Harbinger. As in 'of doom'."

For Terry, the only positive residue of the whole dreadful relationship was sitting in the back seat, leaning out of the car, lips and ears flapping. The Yorkshire Terrier, Jack Russell cross. He was Terry's part of the settlement. He got the dog, Bragi. Nice name. Her choice.

The music snarled to a stop. Terry pressed eject on the stereo but to no effect. Haakon leaned forward with a helpful observation. "You have chewed the tape," he said.

Imre poked at the stereo, trying to eject the cassette. "Sorry Terry, never happened before. I'm sure we'll get it out."

"Is that the one Inger made?" asked Haakon.

"Yes, it was."

"I thought you were a good match," said Haakon. "Apart from the, you know, wellness issues."

"She was the first to say she's not perfect." said Terry.

"Actually, no she wasn't," said Imre. poking a key into the slot. "That's one of the issues with narcissism."

Imre applied force, stopping as he heard the snap of plastic giving way. "You've broken it," Haakon observed.

Haakon had a literal mind and an aptitude for stating what you already knew. He would be the first to say that you'd broken your skis after you'd been in a collision. He caught Terry's eye in the rearview mirror. "You should get back in touch, it's never too late," he advised.

Terry looked somewhat taken aback. "It is for that one. It's not retrievable in the slightest, rather like my cassette."

Imre turned on the radio, which crackled and hissed between fractions of music. "You may find reception could be tricky," added Terry, "being as we're surrounded by mountain rock in the world's longest tunnel and the aerial's broken."

Imre looked up. It was growing brighter as they approached the exit. "Ah," he said. "Maybe there's hope after all."

The radio crackled into The Hives, "Hate To Say I Told You So", as they drove out of the tunnel into mountainous Nordic countryside. Imre rubbed his trousers and looked in some discomfort. "Ah at last. The scenic route. Pull over when you get the chance."

"Circulation issues?" asked Haakon.

"It would be good to stretch the old legs a little."

"It's your trousers," said Haakon. "Drainpipes went out with The Strokes. Even hipsters wear comfortable slacks for travelling."

"That's very helpful and good to know. I'll make a note of that."

Terry looked around at the splendid scenery, a kaleidoscope of geography after the dark tunnel. "This is the land of the mountain king. Ibsen country. 'To live is to war with trolls in the olds of the heart and mind.'"

Haakon sensed a seam of derision to be mined. "Surely you don't believe in trolls, do you?"

"I tend to take an open mind on such things. Who's to say."

Imre's legs were now in the first throes of cramp, and mythological speculation wasn't top of his agenda. He noticed an opportunity to stretch his legs. "Look, there's some parking up ahead."

"There are stories from my in-laws in Lofoten that are not easily dismissed," said Terry.

"I've family up there too," replied Haakon. "Very distant relatives. 950 kilometres to the north," he clarified.

Terry noticed Imre was in some unease. "Perhaps you might consider trying a kilt for a long journey?"

Imre bore the comment as gracefully as possible but was irked by the critiques of his menswear. Especially coming from Terry whose inability to predict popular trends had led to their least successful expo to date. "It's not a style issue," he grimaced "It's just a twinge of cramp."

"They're said to be very warm in the winter. Lots of men do it, especially steam punks." Terry looked to his right, flipped the indicator. "This will do. Nice spot."

The car pulled over by the road on a grass verge next to thick woodland, rolling down to a fjord. The three men disembarked and soon the idyllic landscape was filled with the scampering and sniffing of a Yorkshire Terrier playing.

Terry fussed with the dog. "Could you get that frisbee in the back? Bragi wants to catch."

Haakon reached to the backseat and handed a well-chewed frisbee across. "Why did you call him Bragi? The god of poetry. Why give your dog such expectations?"

"It wasn't my first choice," replied Terry, "in fact I don't remember my opinion being canvassed at all. Inger was the ambitious type. Aim high I suppose."

Terry threw the frisbee for Bragi, which veered off towards the woods. Bragi ran after it and jumped, hanging in the air for a moment as he caught the frisbee. As he landed, he noticed a rabbit just outside the woodland. The rabbit stood frozen for a moment, then ran off, zigzagging into the woods, Bragi dropped the frisbee and gave chase.

He ran through the woods, darting over logs and mossy rocks as the woodland got thicker. The rabbit took a giant leap over a patch of leaves, which Bragi bounded onto. The leaves and detritus collapsed and, with a tiny yelp, a surprised Bragi fell.

Bragi landed on soft earth and leaves. Looking around, he saw he was in a sizable cave with a patch of light streaming through a small hole some 20ft above. There was an underground stream flowing through the cave. On the far side from where he had fallen he could make out a rough-hewn tunnel, from which the deliberate sound of heavy footsteps were approaching.

Bragi hid in the leaves. He could hear footfall and sniffing nearby but when he dared to peek through the jumble of leaves, there was nothing to be seen. The noise retracted down the tunnel, growing fainter as the dog lay stock still in his hidey place beneath the foliage.

Terry and his friends had been searching though the dense tangle of woods, whistling and calling for Bragi with no joy.

"Look," said Imre, hauling himself through an especially thick thicket, "it's dark in a few hours, let's hang close to the car. Surely he'll pick up our scent and head back?"

Haakon agreed. His boot cut Wranglers had grown distempered and he was inclined towards simpler terrain. "If we turn up the radio, honk the horn, he's bound to hear it. Maybe waft some dog food too. He's bound to be hungry."

"Seriously," remarked Terry. "Waft dog food? One part in a million?"

Haakon appreciated it was a long shot, but they were getting nowhere as it was. "With the right gust of wind, it could work," he said. "Unless the awkward little beggar's stuck in a rabbit hole somewhere."

Terry stared thoughtfully out into the woods, scanning for sound or movement. Besides the occasional sway of a branch, it was still. "Surely we'd hear something if he was," he said. "No, something's up."

"He could be quietly tracking a rabbit?" suggested Haakon, as constructively as possible.

"No," said Imre, "he's about as stealthy as a dizzy elephant. His food's back at the car, my guess is we hang tight and he'll come bounding out."

"You're probably right." Terry took a final look around before reluctantly heading back.

Bragi sneaked out from under the leaves. He noticed barefoot three-toed footprints leading out and back down the tunnel. He looked up at the cave entrance. There were rugged hand and footholds in the wall, and a number of vines and tree roots. He half heard a hiss emerge from the stream, a quick glance but there was nothing there. He fixed the walls with a determined stare. Leapt to the first paw hold. Started climbing.

Bragi reached the top and put his paws over the edge, panting. He heard the radio in the distance, and his tail wagged. Behind him rose a spectral form, indistinct, coiling, serpent like. It nipped Bragi by the back of the neck. Bragi's paws slipped as he and the apparition disappeared back into the cave.

Back at the roadside the men stood at the edge of the woods watching, with varied intensity, with the car radio on full. Beneath them in the fjord they heard an explosion. The men were startled and their eyes followed a parabolic trajectory. Bragi was launched high through the air leaving a smoke trail, landing in a tree near the roadside.

Haakon was shocked, as well he might, having witnessed a dog being ejected from the lake like a ballistic missile. "What in heaven's name..."

Terry rushed to the tree. "Hang on boy. Hey. Could you give me a leg up? Poor lad's stuck."

Imre clasped his hands for Terry's foot and helped hoist him to the lowest branch. "Good grief man, your dog's smoking."

Terry climbed fast, towards a gently smouldering Bragi. "You alright? Let's have a look at you..."

Imre looked on. "It's like something threw him out of the fjord."

Haakon caught up to the other two. "There's electric eels in these waters. Maybe your dog's carrying static?"

Terry looked at him. "Not to that extent."

Imre stood at the bottom of the tree, speculating. "They say there's the spirit in these fjords. Every thousand years it takes a passing traveller, a human form to stride the Earth."

"Does my dog look like a human form to you?" came a slightly irritated voice from above.

Imre took a good look at the Yorkshire terrier in the tree, faint curls of smoke still wisping from his fur and the tips of his ears. "He looks a bit surprised to be honest," he replied.

"So would you in the circumstances," Haakon remarked.

Terry reached the dog. He lifted him gently from a branch and carried him down the tree. "Right, done all we can do for him here. Let's get the little guy straight back home. Imre, no more comfort breaks. Can you fetch me a blanket? The poor thing's in shock."

Imre brought a blanket and they swaddled the dog, his face sticking out the top like a furry child. Haakon looked on approvingly. "Ready as an egg. It's not far. We'll make haste like a flying hammer."

Terry threw him a taut glance as he carried Bragi back to the car.

Across the fjord, the hand of a mysterious creature moved low lying branches out of the way for a better view. It noticed a couple of ravens take off in the distance, The creature closed the branches slowly so as not to be seen. It had gonk-like hair and a long nose.

The ravens Hugin and Munin were in conversation mid-flight. Hugin had a small patch of white feathers on the nape of his neck. Munin was the larger of the two, as black as night. Hugin pursed his beak and thought how best to put it. "Odin's not going to be pleased," he said in a tone feathered with nuance.

Munin tilted his head towards Hugin. "That's an understatement. He'll be about as happy as a frog up a pump. Are you going to tell him?"

"Not keen. You're the diplomat."

Munin mulled over the options for a moment. "In all honesty I think not saying anything would be a good idea. I'm all for being particularly low key in the circumstances."

"Loki? Are you mad? If we talk to him and the boss gets wind we'll be hors d'ouevres."

"Low key, I said low key, not Loki," explained Munin. "But really, I don't think we've got that long to worry about enjoying life."

"We could start with 'don't shoot the messenger...'"

"That would be getting off lightly. Odin isn't known for his mild mood swings and outbursts of leniency."

Hugin looked to Munin, conspiringly. "Let's just not tell him. We're the eyes and ears of the world, how's he going to find out?"

"I like your thinking. And Loki's not such a bad idea either. If you follow the car, I'll stop by the Prince of Tricksters, and we meet up for the afternoon debrief as usual. If we play this one right we might go out with a bang."

"Not literally I hope."

"In a good bang kind of way. Look leave it with me. I've got a feeling our luck's about to change." Munin gave Hugin a knowing wink and peeled off on another bearing.

Loki was strung out. He had his ankles and wrists tied and was laid flat; his weight supported by three boulders. Overhead, curled around a wrought iron pendant, a large snake dripped venom. This was caught in a bowl held by Loki's wife, Sigyn, a fair-haired lady in a white toga whose attentive demeanor concealed a cunning mischief. In terms of sleight and devilry she was much like to Loki himself, but better at it.

Loki was a somewhat older spouse, with the physique of a man who'd been tied to a rock for many months. He was dressed in a naturalist fashion with the pelt of a small ferret covering his modesty. Loki watched nervously as the bowl was close to overflowing.

Sigyn emptied the bowl on the floor and replaced it over him, timing it with the drips and moving as quickly as possible. Still a drip of venom hit Loki. He shook and the cave shook with him. When Loki shook it took on a geological significance, whether minor tremors (when he was holding it together) to major Richter scale activity when he was more irritated and theatric.

As his tremor passed, he looked across at his wife, who seemed to be subtly amused by his torment. "Have you thought about getting a bigger bowl?"

"If only I could. I would love to but you know how Odin is," she said, her voice laden with sympathy.

Loki looked around, taking in his circumstances. They were already pretty bad. "Screw him," he replied.

Sigyn stroked Loki's hair, looking at him with affection. "Did the earth move for you, my darling?"

Loki looked away from her, flopping his head to one side. "No," came his terse reply.

"Aw, don't say that. Where did the romance go my love?" she cooed.

The snake cleared his throat and leaned forwards slightly as if to interject. He spoke in a slow lisp. "So sorry to interrupt. If you had some corks maybe that would solve the dripping issue?"

"It is a shame there are no corks in this cave," she said. Her voice was compassion incarnate, although the snake knew what she was like and her manner suggested she had not looked particularly hard.

Munin flew in and landed at the cave's entrance. Sigyn looked up, "Hello, is this a visitor?

"Leave it love," said Loki, "if this venomous snake was not enough do I have to endure my wife's sarcasm?"

Munin hopped forwards and dipped in a brief bow, like a twitch but with courtesy. "Greetings, Lord Loki."

Loki turned his head, all grievances forgotten with his smile a mask of contrived conviviality. "Munin, or Hugin, what a pleasant surprise, come closer, let me see you."

Munin approached tentatively. "Closer? You're not feeling hungry Lord Loki?"

"I can assure you you're perfectly safe." Loki couldn't be more charming, quite at odds with his aggrieved condition. "You haven't got any cork have you?"

"I'm afraid not, but I do have some news. The Midgard Serpent has escaped his bonds and once again walks the Earth."

A glimpse of hope entered Loki. "My son. Does he come for me?"

"Not yet. His strength will grow but for now he has taken a host and walks the Earth as a dog."

Loki became enthused at this turn of good fortune, with genuine cheer succeeding his front. "The hound of Asgard? A mighty beast with blood on his lips, like Fenir?

Munin shuffled slightly uncomfortably. "Not exactly."

"Still, wonderful news... Does Odin know?"

"I had an idea to visit you first, I thought it might be - expedient? And you know much about diplomacy, perhaps you could advise how I could best tell him?"

Loki's voice became the very epitome of gravitas. "I feel strongly that discretion is by far more valuable than candour in this matter. You did well to tell me first. The dog must be protected until I can reach him, then perhaps the end may not be so final, for both sides."

"That's quite an interesting proposition, but does it not work both ways? Why should not Asgard have the advantage of a swift action?"

Loki had a keen sense of corruption and enjoyed nothing more than a nefarious compact. "I'll put it like this. In return for your silence there must be something you desire? Should this be the world's end you may as well enjoy yourself."

Loki showed Munin a vision. A raven was drinking champagne surrounded by doting doves in the back of a limousine.

"If you help me prevail, your hedonistic raven pursuits will continue tenfold, getting your dirty little raven Ragnarocks off till you've had quite enough. Or you can return to Odin's shoulder and we can all perish."

Munin put on his best poker face. "I think we can come to some arrangement." He gave a dirty ravenesque laugh, they all laughed. The snake dripped venom on Loki. He shouted and the cave shook again.


Bragi was out for a walk in a local park, off the leash and running about. He sniffed around a couple of trees and found one to do his business against. Bragi bore a hole right through it, much to Terry's surprise.

Another dog came across to play and Terry was a little anxious what might happen. Rather than caper around as he would normally do Bragi stood his ground and made a somewhat otherworldly growl. He appeared to have dropped an octave and to Terry's ears seemed to have an almost serpentine quality.

The visiting dog yelped and ran off. Terry called Bragi over and the dog was all sweetness again, though as a precaution Terry put him on a lead.

They walked down a path lined with flowers, and Terry heard light footsteps approaching. He turned around and noticed the flowers had wilted on either side behind them. Looking up he saw a couple of girls had come up to pet the dog.

"Oh, he's lovely, what's his name?" asked Heather.

Terry was a little distracted by the dying flowers lying in their wake. "Bragi," he said.

"I'm Isla," said her friend. "Does he mind if I pet him?"

Terry looked at his dog, he seemed quite placid. "Er. No."

Heather was slightly cautious. "Does your dog bite?" she asked.

"No," he replied absent mindedly.

As Isla bent down to pet Bragi, his eyes glowed red and he nipped and growled at her. She jumped back, "I thought you said your dog doesn't bite."

Terry was shocked and apologised, dragging Bragi away by his leash. He looked at the dog quizzically. He was back to normal and wagging his tail. Terry found himself thinking aloud. "That is not my dog."

Terry left the park and hurried home, with Bragi quite happy to have a jaunty walk. Terry lived in shared accommodation with Imre and Haakon. It was an economical solution to having lost the house and besides, it generally worked.

Being a bachelor in a house share wasn't quite how Terry envisaged his 40s, yet there was staid sociability to the arrangement. They were all in the same business with the same aspirations. All enduring a pre-successful period, as Imre liked to put it.

Imre and Haakon were sitting on sofas, as Terry and Bragi entered the house. They noticed something was bothering Terry. "Is everything OK?" Imre asked.

"Yeah sure, just a normal walk in the park." He let the dog off the leash. Bragi gave a bark and walked out of the room.

Haakon watched him go and leaned forward. "We were wondering if we might be able to talk to you about Bragi?"

"Yip, sure what's up?"

"I think there might be something wrong with him?" said Haakon.

"Granted he's been a little shaken since the incident." Terry was a little defensive, although he'd noticed a couple of small signs himself that all may not be right.

Imre offered his opinion. "He's a little bit more than shaken, more like a complete personality change."

"Don't be ridiculous," he scoffed.

Imre continued. "Hear me out. Your dog's not normal. I've never known Bragi to have mood swings like this before. Yorkshire Terriers are normally quite placid at home. Your dog has the hubris of a gorilla."

"Guys. It's just the time of the year. In heat. Happens with dogs."

"But he's a he."

Terry took a seat in an armchair. "Whatever, leave him alone. He's had a tough week."

Imre looked at him sincerely, "And don't think I haven't heard the voices. Your dog growls in tongues. You've heard him. It sounds like he's cursing in Old Norse."

"Oh," remarked Terry, "and you're a historical linguist, right? This isn't Valhalla Rising. It's a bloody Yorkshire Terrier."

Bragi trotted back in and sat at Terry's feet, observing Imre and Haakon. Haakon was slightly uncomfortable and tried to take the heat out of the discussion, as if a child had just walked in on a family argument. "Look, we really think there may be something up with him, but if you want, we can just park it there. Your dog, we're just trying to help."

Terry reached down and stroked Bragi, who continued his icy stare. It was the stare of a fox looking at chickens, planning which one he'd eat first when the opportunity arose. "So... next week. In terms of help, I could really do with a dog sitter. Don't want to put Bragi in a kennel. I think he's had enough upheaval in the last few weeks."

Haakon was stunned. "You're not still going on that date, are you?" he said.

"Sorry dude. Your dog's a psycho. He needs professional counselling," added Imre.

"You think he needs a psychiatrist?"

"More like a bloody exorcist," replied Imre.

"I'm not convinced he's completely well, at the very least." said Haakon. "Look, she won't be the same as the profile. They never are. Everyone's got at least one good photo where they're dateable."

"It's all booked. Flight's non-refundable. I may as well take a chance. Maybe you could be excited for me for a change? This one could be a keeper."

Imre erupted. "For who? FK Haugesund? Well, I'm not looking after Bragi. He's creepy these days. Sorry Terry, but I'm leaving well alone."

"He's just had a shock that's all. It'll take him a while to settle down. By the time I'm back he'll be right as rain."

Just then, Bragi's tummy made a deep resonant rumble, like faraway thunder. Imre looked sharply at Terry. "What's next... ectoplasm?"

"Did you hear that?" asked Haakon. "I'd take a second opinion if I were you."

"I'd have him collected by the Roman Catholic Church! I'm sure they've got a special pound in Rome for devil dogs. Right next door to 'Budgies possessed by Beelzebub!'"

Haakon tried a different tack. "Who's this woman you're meeting anyhow?"

"She's a nice girl," replied Terry cagily.

Imre had heard enough. "Did you mention in your profile you've got a dog which may or may not be supernaturally active? I think you're on a winner there."

Terry stood up to leave, "No harm in asking chaps but you're right, he'll be fine in the kennels." Bragi gave the guys one more dirty look then trotted after him as he headed towards the door. "The flight boards this afternoon so I'll best take him round. Finger's crossed guys, she might be a bit special."

In the study of a smart country house nestled within the landscape of northern Norway, Naglfari, a costumed Nordic death metalist, was having his tea. His spikey shoulder pads and rubber chest plate had been part of his wardrobe for so long, it was rumoured he never took them off. In fact, he took them off at night to change into his pyjamas and wore fresh ones in the morning. Naglfari had a rail of identical items in his wardrobe and a substantial dry-cleaning bill.

The look had become as comfy to him as a pair of slippers, although this style didn't extend as far as the décor. Naglfari had been at the top for a long time and his success was reflected in the refinement of his home. He had become rather the aristocrat, a knowledgeable antique collector - and an avid enthusiast of Munch, whose more fraught moments adorned the walls.

An attentive PA was with him. "So, it's the smoked salmon, dill and lemon pate?" Naglfari flicked through the menu and looked up over his reading glasses, nodding his approval. "And the band, same starter?" she asked.

"Absolutely. Let's keep it simple. Choice is just an ecological tax on the planet we can ill afford. Oh and some black roses for the dressing room." Naglfari seemed pleased with his choices and tucked the glasses behind his breast plate.

The PA, a music professional in her 30s, gave a brief toothy smile. "How lovely. A nice touch, I'll get it ordered."

As she left, Munin arrived at the window. He knocked his beak on the glass. Once, twice, three times; a stately bird requesting an audience.

Naglfari noticed him. "Most peculiar," he muttered as he crossed the room and opened the window. Munin hopped in and flew across to his desk.

He attempted to open Naglfari's laptop with his beak, but struggled and failed, then looked to Naglfari with a squark.

"Shouldn't you be looking for worms? Or... are you looking for cyber worms perhaps?" Naglfari was amused at himself. He opened the laptop and Munin hopped onto it, then tapped out a message with his beak. Munin was an accomplished typist and the words flowed onto the screen.

'Greetings from Lord Loki. Apologies he cannot speak with you in person but he is detained, situation normal. The good news is...' Munin paused for a moment and seemed to have knocked himself dizzy on the keys, Naglfari offered him a sip of some sparkling water from a tumbler and the raven appeared refreshed. He continued, 'The Midgard Serpent is out and about, his spirit inhabiting the body of a dog as he grows stronger.'

Naglfari leaned closer, reading the screen with his glasses perched on his nose. "At last, great news, great wonderful news. A dog, that's an unusual vessel. What breed, a monstrous wolf like Fenrir?"

Munin gave him a look, wondering if an answer was completely necessary. The tappity tap of the raven's beak on chiclet keys continued. 'A Yorkshire Terrier - black and gold. Yes, I know, not ideal. We'd appreciate some discretion on the matter.'

"Naturally. How long till Ragnarok begins?"

'About two months, given everything goes on track.' The bird looked to the tumbler and back to Naglfari. 'Don't you have anything stronger?'

"Charcoal filtered fjord water gathered in hemp weave buckets. I don't touch anything else," Naglfari enthused. "Drink up it will do your guts a favour. Not long to go, eh?"

Munin scrutinised him for a moment then started again at the keyboard. 'Why are you so positive about the apocalypse?'

"The band's not going to last forever. And neither is nihilism, it's a dying art and besides it always was a young man's game. It's actually quite refreshing to be part of something."

Munin was rendered open beaked by the idiocy of the man. 'A message for my Lord Loki?' he eventually asked.

"Sorry to hear about the continued situation and hope you're as comfortable as possible. See you soon."

'The dog belongs to a Mr Terry Chadwick of Slemdal, Oslo,' said Munin. 'Keep it safe.'

"Is there a postcode?"

'I work off road signs. Do I look like I have GPS? Thanks for the drink.' The raven knocked the tumbler off the table. It smashed. He hopped to the window and launched himself into the sky.

"Anytime. Safe flight." Naglfari reached for the phone and tapped in a number from memory. "Are you still in Oslo? I've got a job for you."


A hairy man took the phone from his ear and put his headphones back on. His tattooed hand travelled from the headphones to a cassette Walkman on his belt. He clicked play and the track 'Personal Jesus' started.

The man wore black biker boots and green overalls, with long hair falling from the back of his baseball cap. He ripped the cord to start a diesel-powered lawn mower and started to cut grass. His colleague was smarter, with a bleached indie haircut, dressed in the same work clothes. On the back of his overalls was the name - Depeche Mowed.

By the time they had finished, the front lawn of their client looked as elegantly striped as Lords on the first morning of a test series. They loaded the mowers in the back of a van, the doors closed revealing a logo and the slogan, 'Barrel of a Geranium'. The men got in the front, with the hairier of the two, Anders, sitting behind the wheel. He took the cassette from the Walkman and put it in the van's tape deck. The track continued, albeit quieter.

"I got the call from Naglfari. It's on," said Anders.

Ketil put his gardening gloves on the dash, thinking for a moment. "The man's a loser, he's more dork than ork. What's on?"

"The Midgard Serpent is free and apparently he's in Oslo."

"No kidding huh?" commented Ketil, fastening his seat belt.

"The host is a dog, I've got the postcode."

Ketil shook his head ruefully. "No women, no kids, no pets. I'm not going to shoot no dog."

"I'll look after the dog, do you think you can clean any mess?"

Ketil looked at him, surprised. "Dog mess?"

"Collateral," clarified Anders. "Unfortunate bystanders, who are unfortunately bystanding in the wrong spot."

"You're going to look after a dog whilst I kill people? That's hardly equitable."

Anders explained carefully. "We'll aim at the others and not at the dog."

Ketil was still thinking about the protruded hotdog with crispy onions he had earlier. "Man, you've got me hungry now. Is this the place?"

They pulled up to Haakon's house and knocked on the door. Imre answered. "Hello guys. Sorry we don't need any gardening."

Anders gave him a hard stare. "Can we come in?" He briefly showed his gun.

Imre processed this for a second. "Sure." He waived them in but Anders gestured he should lead the way. They followed him in.

Haakon was sitting with his back to the door watching TV. "Who was it?" he asked.

"It's a couple of gardeners. They really want to mow our lawn." Anders hit Imre over the head with the butt of his gun, then grabbed Imre and put the gun to his head.

Ketil drew his weapon. "Get the dog and bring him here."

Haakon was on his feet but with the sofa safely between himself and the men, "You guys aren't gardeners."

Anders clicked the safety off on his gun, still pointing at Imre's head. "We kill weeds. Weeds like you. We also do lawn maintenance and hedge topiary but that's more of a sideline. Go fetch the dog. I'll count down from 10. 10..."

"He's not here," said Haakon, who interjected hard on the heels of the 'n' of ten.

"What do you mean, well where is he?" shouted Ketil.

"I don't know."

"9..."

"Ok, he's in the kennel." Haakon's resolve had cracked like bad glaze on a cheap vase.

"Don't tell him anything," said Imre, seemingly unaware that Haakon had already done so. Anders hit Imre over the head again with the gun butt. "Ow," he continued.

"What's he doing in the kennel?" asked Ketil.

Haakon spoke fast. "His owner went to London on a date and he put the dog in a kennel."

Ketil looked confused. "He's going to a lot of trouble for a date. Is he desperate?"

Haakon shrugged. The reality was that Terry was very much on the slope towards desperation, and although these men were threatening them, their assertation stood up. Imre looked over at Ketil, "It's the truth man."

Anders hit him on the head again. "Ow!"

"Shut up." Anders turned to Haakon, "Could you get me the address of the kennel please?"

"I don't know it."

"8..."

Haakon was increasingly edgy and cracked a little further. "Seriously I don't know it, there's not many kennels in Oslo though. Phone round, he's called Bragi."

"Like the god of poetry? Really? Dumb name," said Anders, who then raised his voice. "Bragi, come here boy - where are you Bragi. I've got biscuits. And a harp." He listened. There's no movement. Silence. "Well that went well. Thanks guys you've been very co-operative."

"So, we're cool then?" asked Imre, feeling the gun withdraw from his head.

Anders conferred with Ketil, "Have you got the bible?"

"Nope - left it in the van."

Anders shrugged disappointedly. After a couple of false starts and some thought he launched into a brief oratory. "Prepare to be pruned." He then shot them both.

"Prepare to be pruned? Is that the best you've got? Are these the last words these men should hear?"

"I know," said Anders. "Look to be honest I don't feel the vengeful gardener passage anyway. It seems egotistical and it's not all about me in this moment..." He gestured towards the fallen.

Ketil was somewhat critical. "You just shot two people whilst paraphrasing scripture into a cheap quip. What could be more egotistical? This is a new low."

He considered the note briefly. "OK. We can work on this later. Let's go find the dog."

Odin was seated on a simple throne. The two ravens sat by his shoulders and Thor stood nearby. Asgard was a place of practicality. More an arrangement of various sized huts, like a badly planned allotment, than a gilded city.

Practical too were the matters at hand. It was the 9.30am meeting where Odin's messengers presented a top line summary. As there was often very little top line, Odin having limited regard for Earth geopolitics, the briefing invariably descended into minutiae. That was unless any frost giants were primed to attack, which they weren't at the moment.

Hugin shifted uneasily from foot to foot, took a breath and launched into the daily report. "Magnus Stoltenberg had his tooth knocked out in a fight in year 3 - a kid threw a lucky punch and the tooth was already loose. Oslo Børs Energy has taken a dip at 1.16, down 0.29%. Bearish. 128 marriages today, 200 kids born. Mortality rate constant: 3 bad souls going to Helviti. 105 regulars entering Helgafjell, and 5 brave warriors for the Valhalla induction at noon."

Odin seemed particularly disinterested this morning. "Nothing about Ragnarok then?"

"Not a great deal, no."

Odin veered towards Hugin, fixing him with his one good eye. "Not a great deal or nothing at all?

Munin answered for him, "Zilch, nothing stirring in any direction on that front."

Odin glared at Hugin a moment longer and the raven became markedly less comfortable. Everyone was uncomfortable. Odin wasn't comfortable either, he was on the verge of severe agitation and that didn't make him feel comfy at all.

Odin addressed the elephant in the room. "The prophecies do place the start of events to be occurring now - if not having happened already. I need a jump on things when they do start. If we nip things in the bud then we can change the future. No prophecy is written in stone."

"They are in the Hebrew tradition," said Hugin, regretting it immediately.

Munin whispered, "shhhh" out the corner of his beak.

Odin continued, "I would like you to focus less on the demographics and more on Loki, Fenir and the Midgard Serpent. Any change in their circumstances or loosening of their bonds, I want to know."

"Yes, All Father," said Hugin.

"Because if I felt you were lying or hiding information from me, perhaps out of fear or perhaps cunning, you have any idea what would happen?"

"That is absolutely not the case." they both said.

"You may be aware that I tend to execute the bearers of bad news and, as such, you may wonder why anyone chooses to give me any bad news at all? The reason is that if I find out you're less than forthcoming, then the situation becomes markedly less desirable, as in fate worse than death. In fact, you may find you're slowly spit roasted by horned conger eels for the rest of eternity."

Munin's feathers were distinctly ruffled, "I don't want to be cooked," he replied.

"Who said anything about cooking?"

"Anything remotely concerning forbearers of Ragnarok will be top of the list." said Munin, sounding as earnest as possible.

"Good. Well go. Get on with it."

They flew out of the nearby window. Odin turned to Thor. "Did that sound like a lot of bull to you?"

"I didn't hear any bulls, just two ravens talking as normal."

Odin wasn't so sure. "Go see what the trolls are saying. They've got their ear to the ground, or at least closer to it. Check in on Loki, if there's any mischief, there's a fair chance he's involved. And one other thing, the Midgard Serpent."

"I shall smash it with Mjollnir and then dodge the venom like this!" Thor leaned back and dropped his shoulder - somewhat clumsily.

"That's as may be," Odin said, far from convinced. "I want you to look under a few stones, rattle a few cages but do so in disguise. Should you encounter the Midgard Serpent and be recognised he may strike and I want to make sure of victory."

"But Father, it will be a very one-sided contest." Thor gave another feint, slow like an ageing boxer.

"Bravery has never been your problem Thor. Dodging venom apparently is. Be undercover, blend in, find out what's going on - do not engage. Do not start Ragnarok without my being there."

"But as what?" asked Thor.

"Women always ask questions, no one will suspect a woman. No one will imagine the God of Thunder to wear such a guise. It is perfect."

Thor's brain took a short detour whilst processing this new idea. As a heroic Viking god, the prospect of gender reassignment was as strange to him as economics to an ostrich. "But Father..."

Odin clicked his fingers and Thor's appearance changed to a beautiful Asgardian warrior. Odin took a moment to assess his handiwork and was pleased with the result, although Mjollnir remained rather large. "You will pass unnoticed, even your own horse won't recognise you. You'll need a name... Sandy. No, you're not a Sandy. Thora, that's it!"

Thora looked herself up and down with incredulity. "I feel a little self-conscious," she said.

"Cunning is called for my girl. You'll get used to it. You're enough to turn a Valkyrie's head, but perhaps Mjollnir could be a touch more lady like. I shall hamr your hammer."

Mjollnir changed into a rock hammer. Thora lifted and examined it, aghast. "With respect Father, I look like a kinky geologist."

"You look like your mother. Now go."

"To visit Loki?", Thor said, with some trepidation. "Dressed like this?"

"He won't suspect a thing." Odin was not convinced he believed this himself but continued. "Say you're on business of the king and take a vessel as a gift. Explain the usual envoy would come but the gift is heavy. Besides, Sigyn is lonely, take her to one side and have a chat, woman to woman. She may be inclined to talk."

"She may not be inclined to stop," protested Thora.

"Sigyn does have a particular talent for malicious gossip. Since marriage, she has not indulged in conversation so much, they torment each other but little more. You may find her a fund of information."

Thora was far from sure about any of this but departed on the mission.

"You may want to work on your walk," said Odin.

Thora stopped in her tracks. "Why would I do that?" she asked.

"A little butch, perhaps?"

Thora tried to take a couple of steps more gracefully, gave up on the idea and then strode off in her usual fashion.


A small Lithuanian in her late 20s sat with Terry outside a London cafe. Her hair was long on one side of her head and shaved on the other. There was a table between them with cups and saucers and a teapot. Terry took a sip and looked at her seductively over the teacup. "Your hair is a little different to the pic."

"Yeah, it's longer on one side," she replied. To be fair, Terry didn't look like his photo either. She had been expecting an entrepreneur. The man sitting opposite looked like a hillbilly who'd staggered from a train wreck.

"Yeah, kind of a Phil Oakey deal." Terry clarified.

Beata looked confused for a second. "Who?" she asked.

"Human League, 'Don't you want me', asymmetrical guy..." He gesticulated, illustrating in a crude mime the kind of haircut Phil Oakey had in the 80s, possible before she was born. She appeared none the wiser.

"So, tell me about yourself," asked Terry. "Your profile was a little terse."

"I'm poly." she said.

"Hi, I'm Terry."

Beata interrupted him before he could continue. "No, I'm poly, I'm married, my husband and I are coming up to 10th anniversary together."

Terry coughed into his tea. "That's lovely," he sputtered.

"And I also have partner. He sleeps with us."

"Smashing. That sounds like a modern arrangement." The date wasn't working out quite how Terry imagined. There was a strong argument that this kind of detail would have been better disclosed before he flew over from Oslo. He was rather stumped. "Big bed then?" he politely asked.

"Just standard double. It's a little cramped. So, I'm ideally looking for relationship with someone with their own place - so I can visit." Beata was not always as direct and did often soften her honesty to give a positive first impression. However, with Terry she felt quite comfortable being herself, because she really couldn't give a damn.

Terry was still couching his remarks in whatever diplomacy he could muster. "Would the chaps notice if you're not there - it may be slightly obvious?"

"They'll probably just have sports night. Beer and dips. You know what men are like."

"I do have an idea. Being one myself."

Beata, noting the hint of sarcasm, felt that may be enough about herself for the moment. "So, what about you? Are you single, any partners?

"I'm pretty much completely single, and no partner, or partners whatsoever, I would definitely know about it if there was. I am divorced though, no baggage - except perhaps the dog".

"You think dog is baggage? I love dogs. Where are you from?"

"Yorkshire originally. Moved to Norway when I got married. Set up a little weaving business for a while, which went into receivership. My ex had the financial sense of a rabbit... but new season, new jumpers. I'm doing really well."

She looked at him curiously. "I thought you said you were nurse?"

"I said I'm Norse. At least I look a little Nordic. Scandi, that sort of thing. How about you? Where's your accent from?"

"Same as the rest of me, I imagine. My husband and I are both from Lithuania. We met at the circus, in trapeze department."

"Oh, that's nice." Terry flicked a glance to a clock over the counter. Time hadn't flown. "Do go on," he said.

"We met every night. I fell for him, when he didn't catch me. Circus joke. Then one night we ran away from circus and came to London. I love trapeze but is not good career if you want to walk after forty years old."

"Of course, who wouldn't. So, what do you do now?"

"I drive tube on Piccadilly line. Next stop, Cockfoster." Beata moved forward, intrigued, "So, what kind of dog is it? My flat is too small for dog. Maybe get budgerigar. Except we leave the window open. Small flat, too many men."

Terry's phone rang. He looked at the screen, it said Kennel. He was not keen on answering. He turned it to silent, put it in his trouser pocket and ignored it. They could both hear it vibrating.

"Are you going to get that?" asked Beata.

"Nope that's fine."

"Go ahead. It might be important." Beata had a talent for sniffing evasion and a natural born tenacity for digging out the truth.

"It's the kennel manager," he said. "I've got my dog in kennels in Oslo. He's a bit neurotic."

Beata struggled for a moment to take all this in. "You've got a neurotic dog? In a kennel?"

"No," said Terry, "I meant the manager is possibly a little highly strung."

"The poor thing, how do you know your dog's alright? He might be poorly. I'd want to know if it was me."

"He's fine."

"Answer it."

Terry took the phone back out of his pocket. He spoke as discretely as possible. "Hi, how are things? All... lovely?

In an Oslo kennel manager's office, a stressed looking gent in his 60s was on the phone. The light shade was swinging and there were signs of poltergeist activity.

"Mr Chapman, I do think it's important that we talk about your dog."

"I think this must be a wrong number."

"Chadwick, sorry. That's right." A pen shot off his desk, causing him to jump. "A little distracted at the moment. We need to talk about Bragi."

Terry was aware of Beata listening intently. "Bragi, yes. How is he doing? There isn't anything wrong, is there?"

Mr Lomstad took a breath and started as calmly as possible. "As it turns out, Bragi is quite an unusual dog. Nice temperament, but I think he's missing a more familiar environment and would like to go home now. Can you come and collect him?"

"I'm afraid I'm still in England. On holiday. Perhaps he just needs time to settle?"

A picture floated off the wall, passing behind Mr Lomstad. "I don't think he needs any more time to settle at all, really. Shyness isn't the issue. Do you have any relatives nearby who can come and pick him up?"

"They're all in the UK, what's the problem?"

"Well... I know this may sound crazy... but the impression I get.... And I'm not saying this lightly... is that your dog may have a ghost... to have a ghost up... it appears to be haunted."

"I beg your pardon?" snapped Terry.

A bulb exploded in the light shade, fizzing sparks. "Mr Chapman..."

"Chadwick."

"Sorry, it's been quite a day. There's no way to put this gently, I think you've got a haunted dog."

"I heard you the first time. What on earth do you mean man... who is this?" Beata was increasingly interested in the whispered fragments of conversation as Terry bristled in quiet indignation.

"This is Thorbjorn Lomstad..."

"If this is someone's idea of a joke I'll report you, and your operation, to the... kennelling association. I don't have time for this. I'm quite busy. Goodbye."

Beata looked at him curiously. "That sounded important."

"Just some crank of a kennel manager. Clearly out of his mind." Terry stuffed the phone back into his pocket. "Sorry, where were we?"

"What did he say?"

"He says my dog has a ghost up... It's haunted, somehow.... It really doesn't matter."

Beata's curiosity was piqued like a cat spooked by a cucumber. "How very strange. Haunted you say?"

"Yes. Mad. Clearly not fit to be running a kennel."

".... Is it possible to haunt a dog? Why bother?"

"I'm sure I don't know. Doesn't matter."

Beata's eyes filled with a rather urgent concern. It was clear to Terry that she really did like animals. "Do you think it's safe to leave your dog in the care of lunatic?"

"I'm sure he's in safe hands. You do have the loveliest hands by the way."

Beata was having none of it. "What's his name?"

"Who? Mr Lomstad?"

"No, your dog, your quite possibly very ill dog, the one which you left to fend for itself, which may be currently being mistreated in hands of lunatic."

"Bragi."

"Like the poet?"

"... Yes."

"Nice. You live an unusual life don't you. Knitting jumpers. Abandoning poorly animals. A potentially haunted dog... called Bragi."

"Possibly more interesting than the usual banker or Transport For London types, I would imagine."

"True. Granted. No harm in occasional circus act I suppose... it's certainly been different afternoon." Beata glanced at her watch. "Look I've got to get going. I teach a Javanese gong playing class at 8. Wouldn't want them to start without me."

"Oh really, Gamelan?"

"Not everyone has heard of it. Do you play?"

"Yip well you know, I dabble... the way you do. Heard a good joke about that once. What do you call a Javanese musician with flatulence?"

Beata smiled, confused. "I don't know."

"Gong with the wind."

Silence. Beata reached for her bag, getting ready to leave.

"You know," Terry said, "that's not my joke of course. Heard it from a comedian. In Jakarta."

"You clearly know all best people. Whereabouts in London did you say you were?"

Terry waved for the waiter to bring the bill. "Actually, I live in Oslo. I'm just in London for a few days. Business."

Beata gulped down her drink. "Weaving business?"

"Well yes, woollens are expanding, knitwear never sleeps." Terry winced at his own remark, and Beata smiled at the cheesy dreadfulness of his repartee. He was clearly not a player and different to the men she usually met through the app.

"You know, if you're around a few days we should meet up."

Terry was astonished. Clearly, he must be smoother than he imagined. "I thought you were rather oversubscribed."

"My husband and partner are in Florence this weekend. Besides, I'm GGG."

"The boxer?"

"No - Have you ever read Dan Savage?"

Terry relaxed a little, he was on firmer ground. "Never read the books. Saw The Da Vinci Code though. Very Tom Hanks."

She smiled a tolerant smile reserved for docile suitors and looked at her watch. "OK, I'm going to my class now. I'm in a play tomorrow night, upstairs in Bar Sappho."

"Is that in the Shoreditch triangle? I'll find it."

"When are you going back to Norway?"

"I'm in town all week, so yes, that would be great! Good. What are you playing?"

"I'm a washed-up alcoholic floosy."

"Oh... you don't look washed up".

"You're a funny guy." It would have been obvious to most people that this was meant sarcastically but Terry took it as a compliment. He battled onwards.

"There's plenty of years left in you... drinks... floosing... hardly a mile on the clock."

Beata motioned towards the door. "Kind."

"I mean, you're barely a cougar."

"That's not appropriate."

"Right." Terry's spectacular burst of improvised wit had come to a natural end.

"OK, lovely meeting you" said Beata, "and see you Saturday... gotta dash, I'll text you."

She stood up and Terry followed. She gave him a peck on the cheek before leaving. Terry was rather dumfounded but delighted. He sat back down at the table, took his mobile out and texted Haakon, 'She's a keeper. "He wrote. "It's all finally looking up.'

Terry wandered outside and started singing the intro to 'Ain't It Kinda Wonderful'. There was the sound of an ukulele which joined in on the second verse.

Terry looked around. "What on Earth is that?" He went to a manhole and bent down to listen. The sound appeared to be coming from there. "Excuse me mate, you alright?"

A voice came from beneath the manhole. "Yeah."

"You're playing music in the sewers?"

"Yip, great acoustics down here. Just good for practicing, in sonic terms it's as good as the Albert Hall. Do you mind if I accompany you?"

Terry had a quick look around; the street was almost empty. "No, by all means. I was just singing a song to myself, didn't realize it was that loud."

"What's the occasion?" the voice asked.

"I've just met a lady."

"Fair enough. Anytime you want to start off, I'll jump in."

Terry had a moment of clarity that he was talking in a reasonably loud voice to a manhole cover. "I'm a tad thrown now." Terry cleared his throat. "Ain't it kinda wonderful. Ain't it kind of fun."

The voice came from beneath. "A one a two a one two three."

"I've started mate. I thought I was doing the intro and you were joining in?"

"Have another go."

Terry started to sing. After a verse he continued his musical stroll down the street, it had been a remarkable day so far and he was enjoying it. He heard a splashing noise from below as the ukulele player struggled to keep up. They got to another point in the song and a double bass started up.

"How many of you are down there?"

"It's more a loose association of musicians than a community really. About a dozen. Less when it's raining."

They continued and reached another point in the song. Some drums kicked in.

"Excuse me, you've got a drummer?"

"Yes, could you mind strolling around a bit slower? It's getting a bit congested down here."

Terry saw a public toilet, one of the electronic ones with a sliding door. He had an idea. Singing as he walked towards it he entered and closed the door. After a moment the loo flushed. He heard a cacophony of startled musicians, a mishmash of voices and the dismal honk of damp woodwind. Terry exited and moved swiftly away but was surprised by a nearby noise.

"Pssst."

Terry scanned the street, there was no one there. Imagined he must have heard something and started walking again.

"Pssst, Terry. Over here."

Terry looked across and down. There were 6 hats floating in the air at around waist height; a black bowler, a wool felt fedora, a baseball cap, a trilby with a grosgrain band, a beret and a pink stetson.

"Yeah that's right Buddy, the hats. Come over here, we need to have a word."

Terry wandered across. "OK. Is this some kind of set up, where's the speakers?"

"No hidden camera, no 'you've been Punk'd', no giant rabbits going to run out and mug you, this is business. We've come to have a word about the dog."

"About Bragi? Who am I speaking to exactly, and where are you?"

"We're under the hats dummy, the name's Morten."

The fedora turned towards the bower hat. "He can't see you," a voice said.

The beret moved slightly in a sassy arc, "He can see the hats."

"Shut it you guys," said Morten. "OK Terry, you've had a strange week, we appreciate that, but we don't have much time and we've come to help. We're tusser."

"Give over."

Morten continued, "It's a kind of troll. We're from Spiraltoppen. We're small, we don't enjoy civic centres, and we're here to get you out of the shit."

"And we're invisible to the human eye right now, which is why you may have some difficulty seeing us," said the fedora.

"Apart from the hats," the beret confirmed.

"Yeah, dummy." The fedora swivelled towards Terry, "Obviously we can't turn our clothes invisible, so we're wearing hats so you can see where you're talking to."

"And it's a bit cold," said the trilby, which shivered in the cool afternoon.

"Standard troll procedure," said Morten. "We're wearing the hats as a courtesy to you. It's better. You can see us, everyone's relaxed, but if things get a bit tasty."

"Or a bit naughty," said Rocky, a somewhat gruff tone wearing a baseball cap.

"It's VWOOMPF... ditch the hats and we're out of here."

"Adios muchacho," said the trilby.

"So," said Terry, "if I'm given to understand this correctly. I'm talking to a group of naked trolls, wearing hats, who want to talk to me about my dog."

"It's not an ideal world," said Morten.

Terry looked around, "Where's Beadle?"

"Who?" said the gruff voice. "I don't think you're listening. You're away with the fairies, keep up mate. Right, you need persuading?"

"Don't do it Rocky," said the fedora.

"Stay outta this Vince." The baseball cap and a series of stampy little footsteps went over to Terry who then doubled over, a look of utter anguish on his face.

"Let go Rock, I think he gets the point," said Morten.

Terry was incredulous. "So, I've just been assaulted by a naked, ball grabbing troll?

"Listen cupcakes," came the gruff retort, "you got to get yourself back to Norway pronto, the situation with that dog of yours is only going to deteriorate."

"I'm on holiday."

The fedora rocked with scorn. "You call this a holiday?"

"We've seen her buddy," said the beret. "Who cuts her hair? Ray Charles? What kind of guy comes all the way from Norway for a blind date?"

The bower thought it through. "I don't know, it's cheap to fly if you book in advance."

"Sssh," came a noise, which could have come from any one of the hats.

The discussion had gone pretty much as Morten expected, that is to say it had veered sharply off message in no time at all. It was time to get back to business. "The Midgard Serpent has escaped," he said. "That thing in your dog is no regular thing. It's of Asgard, Loki's spawn. The next and final meeting between it and Thor is predicted to occur at Ragnarok, when the Serpent will come out of the fjord and poison the sky."

"My dog's just got indigestion."

"Now, how it got out of the fjord surprised even us," continued Morten.

"And we get around," said the fedora.

Aside from the pain he recently endured via the hat named Rocky, it occurred to Terry he was either dreaming or that Beata had put something in his tea. In all likelihood it was the latter. However, whether psychoactive manifestation or not these floating hats were potentially dangerous and were best handled with tact.

"Must dash," he said. "Let's talk about this another time."

"It has to be you who tackles the Serpent. But you must decide to do so yourself. We can help you to defeat this Asgardian aberration."

"You can rip its freaking guts out," said Rocky.

The stetson sidled towards the cap to have a quiet word. "Did you know you're kind of passive aggressive? You're giving trolls a bad name."

"Hey, I'm not the problem. You've seen Troll Hunter? They're nasty. I'm just a victim of the media."

"We appreciate this is all a bit unusual," said Morten, persevering.

"Just a bit. I've been writing to this woman for weeks, if I don't turn up at the show it's screwed."

"I'm not sure this scenario of the entire sky being turned to poison has fully registered with you."

"To be honest," argued Terry, "I don't see how a small terrier is ever going to be in a position to turn the sky, as in the sky of the entire planet, to poison. A room, fair enough. What do you think the cubic capacity is of a small dog? If I were you, I'd take another look at the numbers."

The trilby spoke up. "You're prepared to turn your back on the planet, to turn up to a theatre, to see a woman, who quite frankly you've got next to no chance with whatsoever, because of a very slim chance you might get lucky?"

"If you put it like that. Yes."

"She's just selling tickets to her show. Literally she's putting bums on seats. That's it."

"I'm not sure I should be taking relationship advice from a naked troll."

"He's got a point," the trilby conceded.

Terry considered Morten's pitch. "What kind of timescale are we on? Are a few days going to make that much difference?"

"Yes." Morten replied.

"Right. Well unfortunately this is not doable. I'm off. Nice meeting you."

"You don't mess with us," said Rocky. "You've got an obligation. You're getting on that plane, capiche?"

"I'm bloody well not doing anything of the sort."

"Rocky, get him," said Morten.

"Hey, hey, get that nebby little freak away from me. Get off!"

Terry swatted away at the air. Clearly perturbed at an imminent assault by Rocky the troll.


An hour later, Terry reached the front of the line at the airport check-in. He moved with mild discomfort.

"Eight seats to Oslo, Fornebu please."

The check-in officer looked around, "But there's only one of you."

"I know. I have proximity issues, prefer to travel in a block."

She squinted cynically at Terry. Dealing with passenger's phobias was a familiar part of the job but this was a new one. He received the tickets and moved through, joining the queue for security. Eventually his hand luggage was passed through the scanner.

"Did you pack your luggage yourself, Sir?" the security officer asked. When Terry conceded that he did, the enquiry progressed as to whether he would mind opening it. Inside were several hats; the officer browsed past the pink stetson to the bowler, and then lifted out the trilby, checking beneath the hatband. "Business trip or pleasure?" he asked.

Terry felt that neither option cast him in a great light but that the latter was less complicated. "Pleasure," he said.

The officer could have sworn he heard a tiny snigger emerge from behind the counter.


Thora arrived at the cave mouth. "Loki, Sigyn – I come with greetings from Odin and I bring you a token of his benevolence." Thora raised her arm and presented a bucket. "It's for catching venom," she clarified. She looked around and saw Sigyn, who was slumped against a rock with her head resting on a hand. She turned her head and it was clear she had been weeping.

"Isn't Loki supposed to be here, tied to that rock?" asked Thora.

"That snake." said Sigyn.

Thora was confused and looked to the snake on the iron pendant who shrugged.

"No, not that snake. Loki, he left me."

Thora was wondering if Loki left with a snake when Sigyn continued. "So, you're rather late with that tribute. He turned into a salmon and jumped in the river, off to spawn I imagine. Most likely upstream if you give a damn. I don't."

"But if he could just escape, why endure the all the dripping venom?"

"Oh, you know what Loki's like. What kind of man gives birth to a horse? A regular guy? Would you like to join me?"

Thora strode towards Sigyn and sat on the wooden bucket so they could have a chat. "I am Odin's envoy, here to bring this tribute which was too heavy for ravens to lift. I go by the name of Thora. As that's my name."

"I see, well Thora, it is good that you go by your name, it simplifies matters. As you are aware, I am Sigyn. Loki could have escaped earlier but it was kind of consensual, and besides if news got back to Odin then it could have been worse. Strange as he is I don't believe death is on his bucket list, no pun intended."

"So, why go now?"

Sigyn leaned in, lowering her voice, "Between you and me..."

"And me of course" the snake pitched in.

"Yes, but you know already. There is word in the air that the end days may be coming."

"Ragnarok?"

Sigyn glanced around surreptitiously and with more than a hint of theatre. "Keep your voice down, yes. Only it may not be quite the end for everyone, perhaps more for Odin than others."

"I see... hmmm...." said Thora, whilst not quite grasping the nuance. "Did he say where he was going?"

"No, and that's why I think he's not coming back, at least not to me. I got the shock of my life. All I saw was a fleshy tail jump around the corner, then 'splash'. It's just plain callous."

"You're worth more than that."

"Thank you my dear, you are a handsome girl, aren't you?" Sigyn wiped away a tear and put her hand on Thora's knee. "Being as the end is coming, it's so nice to have a friend."

Thora was somewhat uncomfortable with the familiarity, Sigyn being her aunt after all, but she pressed on with the mission. "This end you mentioned. During the final battle, Fenir is prophesied to eat Odin. But isn't he still bound with fetters?"

"There is another, the hound of Asgard is in play."

"Another monstrous wolf? To bring the world to darkness and unleash chaos?"

"Apparently, not exactly. Our agents have tracked him to the Lomstad Doggy Daycare and Luxury Kennel in Oslo."

Thora squeezed Sigyn's hand and gently removed it from her leg. "Must be off," she said.

"Aren't you even going to stay for some soup... and a roll?" asked Sigyn, with a coquettish wink of her eye. Or it could have been a tick, Thora wasn't sure.

"You're kind but I'll spare you the trouble." Thora rose and headed towards the cave mouth. "Sorry about your husband," she said.

Sigyn's lips flickered briefly with a mischievous smile. She gave Thora a knowing nod. "Give that devil my regards if you catch up with him."


It was midnight. Anders and Ketil were taking cover around a corner. They sat and reloaded, pinned back with the occasional bullet whistling past.

"Invisible guards," said Anders. "Invisible bloody guards packing Smith and Wesson revolvers. What kind of kennel is this?"

"If they're invisible, why can we see the guns?"

"Maybe it just affects organics."

"So, they're naked?" Ketil shouted round the corner, "Perverts!" and was met with a hail of gunfire.

Anders reloaded, grimacing ruefully. "I struggle to see how this is acceptable. In fact, this is heading very quickly towards being an entirely unreasonable situation. I know this is Scandinavia but come on. Naturalist gunmen? They're probably Dutch."

"Not necessarily men either, they could be naked women, packing vintage heat. Maybe they're invisible as they're shy?"

Anders shook his head ruefully. "I am a very liberal individual and when it's my time let it be to a naked Dutch lady with an antique firearm, but I strongly suspect that they are not ladies in any sense I would recognise. Let's see." Anders shot at a fire extinguisher - it exploded. He broke cover and fired at a couple of figures flecked with foam. He hit both, they fell - though one figure shot back. Anders was hit and slumped to the floor. Ketil hurried over.

"Dude, dude, hold on... you'll be OK." Ketil looked over to see two naked trolls lying on their backs, with gunshot wounds and big noses pointing up into the air. "What are those things?"

An electrical crack and lightning spread across the corridor, triggering the locks on the cage doors. All the dogs were released and ran off. Thora burst through the roof and landed in a crouch.

"I've seen everything now," said Ketil.

He fired the gun at Thora who deflected the bullets by swinging her rock hammer. She took in the scene. "I understand you are looking for the dog and have slain my troll associates. Where is the dog?"

"I don't know," said Ketil, fairly honestly.

Mr Lomstad arrived in a fluster. "Who let all the dogs out? What are you doing here, are you a gardener?" He gestured to the corridor, with its empty cages and dead foam covered trolls. "This is carnage - I'm calling the police." He glared at Thora, "This is a kennel not a cosplay convention. Stop the dogs!"

"I'm looking for a Yorkshire Terrier called Bragi."

"Oh, that little creep, I should have guessed he'd have something to do with it. I dare say he's gone with the rest."

They hurried into the yard. A small hole was burned into the wire fence, still smouldering, through which the dogs had escaped into the city beyond.

Thora was not pleased. "Show me the dog's cell," she ordered. Mr Lomstad, who, startled by her abrupt tone felt his hackles rise. There was something in Thora's demeanor though that deterred him from passing comment, and he turned and led the way. As they left the yard and returned to the facility Thora turned to Ketil and explained quite plainly that he was, "in so much trouble it was unbelievable."

Ten minutes later, Thora took a dog blanket and closed the cell door. Ketil was inside the cell sitting with hands and legs bound. The name plate about the door read, 'Bragi'.


At the arrivals gate at Fornebu, a scattering of chauffeurs held signs for various business passengers. Somewhat lower down a cardboard sign, seemingly floating a foot above the ground, carried a single name, 'Terry'.

Moments later, Terry was in the airport carpark, waving a series of undetectable trolls into his car. The engine grimly turned over then eventually lurched into life, and the radio clipped into 'Gimmie Shelter'. Terry turned the music down a notch, "Are you guys comfortable in there?" he asked.

"Yip, we're good," said Rocky. "Nice ride."

"How did you get to the airport?"

"We  hitch... We jump on lorries usually."

"Or take the train," said Morten.

"You're the fedora, if I remember?"

"No, I'm the fedora. I'm Vince. Loving the Lada by the way."

"Sweet."

"Terry, I'm Olaf, your airport pickup. Guys I've got some news, we've got an interested party waiting in Slemdal. I'll explain when we get there."

"What's with the music policy?" asked Morten.

"There are other stations. Help yourself. The tape's jammed."

"No, this is good. Usually trolls like Stones," said Rocky. "Living under them, listening to them, sometimes eating them. This is the good bit..." Rocky started to sing in falsetto. Other trolls joined in on the chorus. Terry abstained but rolled the windows up so no-one would overhear and think it was him.

They eventually came to the suburbs and parked in a residential area. Thora was outside on the pavement waiting.

"OK," said Olaf, "this is the place. We won't go inside though."

Terry couldn't help but notice the attractive, strangely dressed superheroine on the pavement. "Who's that?"

"That's not my favourite person. He's known as dwarf kicker to my people, and anyone who kicks a dwarf into a fire is one mean devil. Some of my larger relatives have had a bit of trouble with this one. Watch yourself, he's got a temper."

"He?" said Terry. "Nah, no way. Really?"

Olaf had heard of Terry's soft spot for the ladies and made the introductions with some apprehension. "Terry, this is... Thora, Thora, this is Terry, the owner of the errant dog."

Thora wasted little time on pleasantries. "You put your dog in a kennel to go on a date. What sort of man are you? Two trolls have died, and the Midgard Serpent is at large."

"Well obviously had I known the circumstances... I'm sorry, who are you again?"

"I am Thora. Of Asgard."

"Ass Guard? That's a deodorant isn't it?"

"I am an Asgardian."

Terry was perplexed. "Good luck with that. I don't know what that involves but I hope it's working out for you. I'm sorry but what's going on?"

"This is the house of Snorri Snakker. He will help us find your dog."

"Snorri Snakker, the dog tracker?" said Rocky. "He's right for the job - he can find any dog with that nose of his - but he's untouchable."

"Why?" asked Terry.

Nobody was in a rush to answer, and it fell to Thora to step forward with an explanation. "He is part troll on his father's side but his mother was, well you'll see for yourself. He is part canine."

"He is despicable," added Morten.

Thora showed a small blue fleece flecked with a paw print design. "I have the dog's blanket. Snorri will track him."

"Am I hearing this right?" said Terry. "There's a troll in that house who's half canine?"

Thora nodded. "Golden retriever. Fortunately, a hunting dog."

"Inexcusable really," said Vince.

"How is this possible?"

Again no one leapt up to elaborate, as tended to be the case in matters concerning Snorri. Thora took a breath and continued. "Inter-species breeding is not encouraged, but it happens in other realms. Sometimes it happens that a god marries a giant. Loki, my father's blood brother - so technically my blood uncle - has lower and more peculiar tastes."

"He turned himself into a mare and gave birth to Sleipnir, Odin's horse. Imagine that, giving birth to an eight-legged horse. No one knows who the father is but it can't have been a nice evening."

Terry boggled in astonishment. "What kind of man wants to give birth to an eight-legged horse?"

"Maybe that's how he gets his kicks," said Rocky.

"Then," said Thora, "he courted an Ogress, Angrboda, they had three children. One night with a retriever is bad enough but - three children by an Ogress? And they're not pretty children. Hel, Goddess of the underworld. Fenir, a giant wolf - and Jörmungandr, also known as The Midgard Serpent, the spirit of whom is currently possessing your dog."

"So I've heard. I've read the Prose Edda; death by Ragnarok, both armies wipe each other out and the world ends - according to a book of old Icelandic fairy tales. Come on. Pull the Edda one."

"Your dog is not mentioned..." said Thora.

"Yes, I know that. It would have stood out."

"And yet here we are."

Terry's phone rang, he looked at the screen and answered it. "Hi Mum - a little busy, can I call you back?"

"Terry, what's happening? I just had a visit from the police. There's been a homicide at your house. Are you safe?"

The news stopped him in his tracks. "Imre or Haakon?"

"Both. They found grass clippings at the scene. You need to contact them for questioning."

Terry was lost for words. His head span. "Tell them I'm overseas. It's important. I've lost Bragi..."

"I'd say Bragi is the least of your worries given the circumstances, turn yourself in to the police. You're a suspect."

"I need to find my dog Mum. It's a strange day - don't worry, I'll explain later."

"Don't worry...??!" Terry cut the call short, turning the mobile off.

"You should lie low, go underground," said Morten. "We'll get you to the dwarves. They bound Fenir, they'll know what to do."

"Haakon and Imre?" said Terry, in disbelief. "What happened?"

Thora mused for a moment. "There's a gardener locked in the kennel. Battle trained. The grass clippings suggest he might know something about it. The other gardener is dead. Shot by trolls."

"They'll both be dead soon enough. I'm going to the kennel. I'll kill that bastard myself."

"We're sorry for your loss," said Morten, "but he'll be in custody by now. It's a crime scene, no place for revenge. As hard as it is, I'd hold that thought for later. Look, the day isn't going to get any better, let's get you underground."

"Where do the dwarves live?"

An unfamiliar voice piped up; it was Mitch with his inner-city brogue. "Where they've always lived, sucker. Frogner Park."

The trolls helped Terry into the car. They drove off at speed. Thora watched them go then walked up the path to the house. The door slowly opened with a protracted squeak. There was a figure covered with a black cloth - the shape was mainly troll but with dog ears and the distinctive shape of a snout. A golden tail wagged at the back.

Having ridden through the night on his customised Harley, Naglfari arrived at the kennel. He picked the lock and snuck in, as surreptitiously as a musician dressed as a dark lord was able. The kennel was unnervingly quiet, and he noticed a distinct lack of dogs. Eventually, Naglfari found Ketil locked in Bragi's cell. He was unimpressed.

Ketil looked up and noticed him, his delight at having been found faded to some trepidation. "We've got a serious problem," he said.

"You're the one with the problem if you haven't got the dog. What happened?"

"What happened is that Anders got shot by trolls and a girl in a role-playing outfit turned up and kicked my ass. Now I'm locked in this kennel."

Naglfari took in his predicament. "You're certainly in the doghouse. Where is he?"

"Escaped. Will that raven you described find him?"

"That raven I described seems to have disappeared."

A voice came down the corridor, catching Naglfari by surprise. "I would say that the raven's whereabouts are the last thing to concern you." Loki approached them, still wet from his recent aquatic episode. He was not pleased.

"My Lord Loki. We were just about to search for the dog."

"You mean he's not with you? Let's see, who's this in his kennel? Is that not his name above the door?"

"Lord Loki, if I may explain..."

"A strange looking Yorkshire terrier I must say, still I've not seen one before. Does he do tricks? Let's see if he can do this one." Loki crouched next to the cage. "Give me your gun, little dog."

Ketil looked terrified, uncomfortably moving his bound hands to his holster. He slowly handed over his gun.

"Now," said Loki, "where is the dog we're looking for?"

"A troll was shooting at us then a woman came through the ceiling..."

"That does sound rather unfortunate... Then?"

"The dog escaped."

Loki, not being familiar with firearms, aimed the gun crudely at Ketil. He spoke aside to Naglfari. "Help me out here. The pointy end goes towards him and the switch is this flap underneath?"

"Yes."

Loki pulled the trigger and was satisfied with the bang. Ketil slumped silently. "Was that a good shot?"

Naglfari was quite mindful of not upsetting Loki further. "It certainly seemed to do the trick," he said.

"Why are you still here, shouldn't you be looking for something? Something dog shaped perhaps? That reminds me."

Loki changed shape into an Afghan Hound with a fine, silky coat. "What do you think, too overstated?"

"I must say, the look does suit you Lord Loki. Is it somehow tactical?"

"Do you know the story of Sleipnir's parentage?"

"I did hear a rumour but naturally I discounted it."

"To bring the Midgard Serpent into the world is the same as any new arrival. It requires romance and an element of seduction. What dog could resist a great bitch like me?" Loki hung his tongue out and panted, his ears keen and his coat slightly damp yet shiny.

"So that's the plan?" asked Naglfari.

"Yes."

"No plan B then?" he double checked.

"Not that I'm aware of."

"Your scheme to bring about Ragnarok is basically Rosemary's puppy?"

"That's Asgard for you. Why, do you not think it'll work?"

There was a slight edge in Loki's voice which deterred Naglfari from any further questions.

"I can't imagine any dog would stand a chance. You look tremendous," he said.

"Thank you, now you know Oslo much better than me, it may have changed since I was last in town. If you were a small possessed terrier, where would you go to relax?"

"Probably east side."

Loki wagged his tail in a couple of elegant swipes. "Good, point me in that direction. Frankly you're little use to me dressed as you are, but you may as well be a decoy to amuse the police."

"I appreciate your generosity in the matter. This way."

They passed Mr Lomstad on the way out. He'd had a busy evening already. "Who the heck are you?" he demanded.

"Do you want to shoot him?" asked Loki.

Naglfari wasn't keen. "Not especially."

Mr Lomstad was rather taken aback by a talking dog ordering his assassination. Loki turned to address Naglfari. "That wasn't a question."

"I've not shot anyone before. I'm a musician."

Loki looked up at him with disappointment in his furry brows. "Might you punch him?"

"My hands are insured for 10 million Krona."

"Do try to impress me."

Naglfari threw the feeblest punch at Mr Lomstad, who fell over backwards with an "Ow."

Loki looked at Naglfari with disdain. Then he turned to address Mr Lomstad. "One of the advantages of being tied to a rock for years is it does make you more stoic. I say let's focus on finding the dog. But if I find out you've mistreated him whilst he's been in your care, I'll kill you myself."

"That sounds very reasonable."

"And if Ragnarok does not go as planned and the world doesn't end in quite the way I prefer - I'll come back and bite your balls off." Loki showed his teeth by way of illustration.

"I'm sure it'll be fine."

"Good." Loki seemed satisfied and turned away, slinking down the corridor like a Crufts champion on a runway. "Come Naglfari, romance is calling."


Thora hadn't quite known what to expect, yet the vision of oddness which opened the door seemed friendly if of peculiar appearance.

"Snorri? Snorri Snakker?" she asked.

"Yes," came a curiously normal if slightly short-winded voice from beneath the cloth.

"You track dogs?"

"Yes, I do." Snorri was pleased to have a guest and ushered Thora inside.

"Are you out of breath? You seem a little panty."

"It's not often I have visitors. Especially from one so beautiful. I myself am not a little panty. Although such items are welcome in my home."

"I would warn you not to flirt with me. That would not be wise. May I come in?"

"Of course, of course... come in, I'm sorry I don't have many guests. I would invite you to sit down but I don't have any chairs. The consequence of an unusual childhood. You see, I was never allowed on the furniture."

"I'll stand thank you. I am looking for a dog."

Snorri's ears pricked up beneath the cloth. "Oh, lucky you! What did you have in mind? Something refined yet exciting... perhaps a Tibetan Mastiff?"

"No, you don't understand..." She regarded Snorri suspiciously. "Are you some kind of pimp? I'm looking for a lost dog, a very important animal - A Yorkshire terrier. Here's his blanket." She handed Snorri a blanket.

He inhaled deeply. Seemed lost for a moment. "Oh nice, very nice. What's his name?"

"Bragi - like the poet of Asgard."

"Really?"

"It's not my dog."

"I don't ask questions. I just find the dogs - for owners, new owners, walkies - each to their own. I get all sorts in here. Far be it for me to stick my nose into your business." He sniffed. "Have you got money?"

"You will be rewarded."

"How did you find me, was it through the website? That's membership only, just you're not the usual punter - sorry client."

"The trolls brought me."

"Oh," exclaimed Snorri, "that is a surprise. My very distant family. I'm rather a black sheep you see, a black sheep dog more precisely. They must really need my help if trolls brought you here. This could be expensive..."

"Money is not a problem."

"And biscuits?" Thora stared at Snorri, puzzled by his words. He snickered, like Muttley with a chest complaint. "No, I'm only messing with you. Trolls brought you, huh."

"The dog went missing from a kennel yesterday evening, a small black and tan Yorkshire terrier."

"Yes trolls. Very cruel people. I left, was discarded actually... like a mongrel, from the pack - and do you know what they sang as the cast me out of the village? 'Who's Snorri now.'"

Snorri broke into song, voice chewed with emotion. 'Who's Snorri now...? Who's Snorri now...? Whose heart is breaking...' And others joined in with harmonies, they were howling along like this 'Arooo, Arooo.' I was a laughing stock. They said, I put the mong into mongrel... but they're not laughing now. Every trog has his day."

"At least you're not bitter."

"Not a bit of it. In fact, it made me stronger. So, tell me about this dog of yours, or... someone else's."

"The owner is wanted for homicide. He was outside but had to leave."

"Nice family. Still, an outcast - I can identify with that. I like him already."

"The dog is host of a malicious spirit, he needs to be found and dealt with."

Snorri cocked his head, "What's going to happen to the dog?"

"There's not a firm plan at present. This is quite a departure from my understanding of events leading up to Ragnarok, we're in uncharted territory. The prophecy says, 'A ship sails from the east, Muspell's followers are coming across the sea, and Loki is steering. There with the Wolf are all the giant sons.' So, it does, as you see, mention a canine - but not specifically a Yorkshire terrier."

"All dogs are descended from wolves," said Snorri, "and many of us keep an element of the wolf within. A terrier you say? I speak all 17 languages of dog, although my Pekinese is a little rusty. You're in luck though. I'm fluent in Terrier. Albeit without a Yorkshire accent."

Snorri sniffed the blanket again. "There may not be much time. At night fall we get started."

"Why wait?" asked Thora.

"I tend to work more at night - you know... for obvious reasons."

Thora considered the obtuse and curious shape of the darkened cloth. "Have you heard of hamrs?"

"Yes, they're very good for hitting things, especially chisels - why?"

"No... hamrs... the ability to change shape."

"A privilege of the Gods, not exactly part of my skill set I'm afraid."

"Sometimes the Gods choose to change other people, especially when it's in their interest." Thora nodded to Snorri and walked towards the door.

"Where are you going?"

"I'm going to see a man about a trog."

Bright light cut the grim atmosphere in Odin's throne room. Thora had finished her recap, which hung awkwardly in the air. Odin raised himself from his throne and started pacing. He hadn't taken it particularly well.

"The Midgard Serpent has escaped? This is ridiculous. I would have known! When did this happen? And you say he is free on the streets of Oslo? He escaped from a kennel?"

"The host is a dog," said Thora, "his whereabouts are unknown."

"A dog, what kind of dog?"

"A small terrier. From Yorkshire."

Odin kicked off. "This is ridiculous. Well, find him!"

"I have a tracker, the best, but he only tracks by night."

"Why is that?" Odin blustered. "He shall track by day and night and shall not rest until the dog is found."

"He's part troll and part golden retriever, mixed parentage - a bit shy."

"Snorri Snakker, the dog tracker? I know of him. A creature so debased he makes Ratatosk the squirrel look respectable... Still, I cannot judge. I've done worse myself." Odin closed his eyes for a moment. "It is done. I have given him form to pass unnoticed. Neither too fair nor foul, able to walk amongst men until he finds our foe."

"Thank you Father. What news of the ravens?"

"They are my eyes and ears but are conspicuous by their absence, they should hurry with this news."

"They seemed a little skittish last time they were here."

Odin bristled indignantly. "They would not dare deceive me - they are surely prey to some darkness and are killed or captured."

At the same moment in Oslo, unbeknownst to them, Hugin and Munin were in the VIP section of the Dirty Bird bar, cavorting with doves to the sounds of gangster rap.

"Just to be on the safe side, perhaps it is wise to check?" said Thora, who was not so sure.

"No, I need you to locate the dog. How many Yorkshire terriers can there be in Oslo? Go now, how hard can it be?"

Terry and the invisible trolls made their way to Frogner Park, and through to the sculpture park at the center. Statues of nudes were frozen into various shapes, sometimes alone but more often in combinations. Dozens of them were piled up into a column in the middle, not so much a scene from Dante as a celebration of form, albeit a curious one.

Mitch pointed with a stick. "It's the lady's navel over here. You might need to bend down a little."

Terry pressed the navel on a naked lady and a hitherto unseen door swung open in the statue, with steps leading down. "Ah, all this time, hidden in plain sight. A doorway to the dwarf kingdom."

"No-one would think about pressing a statue's navel to open a door, most races have doorbells or knockers. Dwarves love stone and live navel high to the world. They appreciate the beauty of both."

"Of course, it makes perfect sense. I never considered that before. Stone navels. Tell me, do gnomes like knees? Do djinns like shins?"

"Are you having a laugh?" said Vince. "There's no such thing as djinns."

"This is no kingdom by the way," said Mitch, "it's more of a city pad - a central hangout. There are deeper levels with a bit more grandeur, but the tunnels are rather small and not for you. You can't change yourself into a rabbit can you?"

"I can't say I ever tried but I'd say it's highly unlikely. Do they know we're coming?"

"Not exactly." Mitch replied.

They turned a corner in the passage and saw a dwarf. "Who the hell are you?" he asked.

"I am Terry and I seek magical help - to a supernatural problem. I am here alone."

"No you're not. I can see trolls you know, you docile long-legged ignoramus."

Mitch spoke up. "What's your name cousin? We mean no harm."

"I am Fjolmir, son of Gandalf, son of Thorin, son of Durin."

"You're having me on," said Terry. "You've taken that from Tolkien."

"You're as ignorant as you look. You'll find Tolkien took that from Sturluson. These are traditional dwarven names as recorded in the sagas hundreds of years ago, which Tolkien borrowed. He was a fan of dwarves and dwarf culture. Except he made Gandalf a wizard. My Dad still gets stick about that. What's your business?"

Mitch stepped in to answer, "The Midgard Serpent has slipped its bonds and now possesses this man's dog."

Terry shrugged, "It appears to be true."

Fjolmir looked confused, "So where is the dog?"

"I left him in a kennel and he escaped."

Fjolmir regarded Terry distastefully. "You're about as bright as belly fluff - you're not related to Tolkien are you?"

"Not that I'm aware of."

Fjolmir turned behind him to another stone door adorned with fresco sculptures. He pressed four navels in a sequence, like entering a pass code. The door swung open. "We've got visitors," he said.

An hour later, inside the troll's reception chamber, three dwarves were sitting on chairs. Terry sat uncomfortably on a small chair, drinking tea from a porcelain cup. There were six empty chairs next to him and an occasional table with a tea set.

Gandalf, a middle-aged dwarf with a two tone beard, was considering the matter at hand. "So, you're saying, presuming you can find the dog, in time, the difficulty is to know what to do with it?"

"That would seem to be the long and short of it," agreed Terry.

The dwarves exchanged glances among themselves. Gandalf spoke again. "You're not doing yourself any favours here, big man. Try that again and you'll be out on your ear."

"No, no," said Terry. "I just meant you're correct."

"Keep your hair on Gandalf," said Rocky, from an empty chair.

"Guys, guys, guys," said Durin, a hard faced elder with braids in his beard. "Come on. Let's think and let old rivalries be past. We clearly need to get the serpent spirit out of the dog. This spirit was bound by water. It came to possess the dog whilst he was found in a fjiord after chasing a froobee?"

"Frisbee," corrected Terry.

"Frisbee," continued Durin. "So how do you take such a spirit from a dog? And how to bind it?"

"Well," said Fjolmir, "Fenir was bound by a fetter our ancestors created. It was as light as a ribbon but the strongest could not break it. We called in Gleipnir and it binds the wolf to this day."

"Would it take long to make another one?" asked Terry.

Fjolmir paused, like a tradesman giving an estimate. "Well it is a big job. You would need the sinews of a bear, the roots of a mountain and the beard of a woman amongst other things..."

"But," said Terry, "a mountain has no roots, and women don't have beards - most women anyway, although it's becoming more popular."

"True, true, but that's just the official version of events. You don't expect us to publish trade secrets, do you? Our kind are too shrewd for that. The breath of a fish stuff was just for the storytellers. It's actually a polycarbonate weave with added feathers, gives it a 'magical' appearance."

Terry considered this for a moment. "PC weave would do it."

"Fortunately, our forbearers made a spare," said Gandalf. "Gleipnir 2 - I've got it in the back somewhere." He hopped off his chair and went to look for it.

Terry watched him leave and heard the scuffing sound of Gandalf ferreting for a fetter, as if it was buried in a junk yard. "Is binding my dog really going to solve anything? The issue is really de-possessing him of this spirit rather than binding him to a rock."

"You can't bind enough dogs in my opinion," said Fjolmir. "Bear with us big man, we're just brainstorming. Anyone else?"

A few moments of concerted silence passed whilst they struggled for ideas. Mitch provided the breakthrough. "How about a laxative?"

Terry sputtered on his tea. "You what? A laxative?"

"Well," continued Mitch, "it seems we've got something inside a dog that we want to get out, why not go for the traditional method?"

"It's not 'a something' inside my dog, it's a metaphysical beast - the spirit of one of the foulest demons around if I'm to understand it right." No-one seemed to be coming up with alternatives and, rather despite himself, he started to give it consideration. "How would you give dog a laxative anyway?"

Durin shrugged. Fjolmir pitched in a suggestion. "How about on a sausage?"

"That's true," said Vince, taking a sip of tea. "Dogs like sausages."

Gandalf returned to the room. "Not easy to do though, he may not wish to be fed. I mean as far as we know he could be flying around firing fireballs out of his... well, you know."

"I'm not sure that I do," said an anxious sounding Terry.

"You know, from the rear quarters, the wagging end."

"Pardon?" said Terry. "Is that likely to happen?"

"Don't listen to him lad," said Durin, "he talks more rubbish than Ratatosk the squirrel. It is a highly unlikely scenario..."

Gandalf gestured towards the feathered contraption he was carrying. "You might have to calm him enough to put him into the fetter. Although the last time we were involved in a fettering the laddie lost his hand."

"His entire hand?" said Terry.

"He's lucky he didn't lose his arm. And he was a god."

"So," said Terry, taking this all in, "if I've got this right the best case scenario is we bind the dog without my losing a hand, give him a laxative and this solves everything. Worst case scenario is he flies around Oslo. How did you put it again?"

"Shooting fire balls from his..."

Terry interjected. "Thank you very much, Gandalf. Classy. So, where does that leave us?"

Vince took another sip of tea. "Given a choice, I'd probably settle for the middle ground."

"I'm not sure what that is," said Terry. "I'm quite attached to my arm. I vote for the laxative."

Fjolmir fixed him with a concerted look. "You will have to give it to him, he trusts you more than anyone, and if there is a trace of your dog left in his demonically ravaged mind, you're the best hope of reaching it."

"I would prefer to know if this fire business is likely before we give him the laxative."

"We've got some sausages in the kitchen," said Fjolmir, avoiding the query. "Durin can bless them to be on the safe side. He'll invoke the dwarven gods, and the god of sausages and meat in general."

Terry viewed the dwarves with some suspicion.


A field in Asgard looked pretty much like a field anywhere. Perhaps the mountains in the distance were a bit more peaky, and the Bifrost set it apart, arcing across the sky like the world's longest rainbow.

Asgardian countryside was also not subject to power lines, wind farms, chem trails, nor especially troubled by industrial farming. It was a bit like an 18th century Lapland, albeit without the reindeer husbandry.

Odin met Tyr and Freyr, both strong warriors, in such a location for reasons of discretion. Odin clasped each in turn and called the meeting. "Thanks for coming, I have news, the day may be approaching."

"I thought it was all rather quiet recently," said Tyr. "Has Loki slipped his bonds?"

Odin nodded ruefully. "As foretold, it has happened."

"I understand it's difficult to escape from enchanted fetters, but surely his wife knows where he is?"

"I asked Sigyn. She said he was going for a walk and would be back in five minutes. Then he turned into a salmon and jumped in the river. She hasn't seen him since."

"I'm impressed." said Freyr, whose voice boomed with precise articulation. "I wouldn't have thought she'd go for that. Do you think she's in on it?"

"I wouldn't have thought so." said Odin. "Sigyn was absolutely fuming. If he survives the battle, he may live to regret it."

"True," agreed Tyr.

Odin looked at the men in turn. "Freyr, what is your readiness for battle?"

"I am just back from my honeymoon and never felt better. My wife is like all the stars in heaven."

"And your sword. The one that fights by itself and has never been bested. Is it still sharp and at your side?"

"I was going to talk to you about this."

"Go on."

"Well," said Freyr, taking a breath. "I kind of exchanged it for my wife."

"The giantess?" asked Tyr.

"Yes. I was very much love struck and it seemed a fair deal."

"Your father in law, the mighty giant king, now has your amazing fighting sword?" said Odin, glowing with a flush of agitation. "Then go and ask for it back."

"It wasn't him," said Freyr, "I gave it to a servant in gratitude for him delivering a love letter. He has now disappeared."

"You pillock," said Odin. He looked Freyr up and down, regarding him as askance as possible with one eye.

"It's OK. I am still ready for battle."

"Oh, you're ready for battle? Have you seen Surt? He is enormous and his sword glows brighter than the sun. How will you best him?"

"With this." Freyr took out a large jagged antler from his belt and held it proudly.

Tyr looked at this in bewilderment. "With an antler?"

"Let me get this straight," said Odin, "You intend to fight Surt with an antler having given away your invincible sword and have married the 60ft woman? How's that going to work? She's 54 feet taller than you, 55 in heels. It's like an emu marrying a canary."

"She is perfect," said Freyr. "As for Surt I could best him with my bare hands, but with this it will be no match."

Odin roared in his face. "With a bloody fire giant, who fights with a burning sword? Freyr, I understand you like tall girls and have been blinded by love, but you really are not helping. Tyr. Tell me you're left-handed."

Tyr raised his right arm. There was a stump at the wrist. "I know what you're thinking. It would have been better to put my left hand in Fenir's mouth."

"Are you ambidextrous?" asked Odin.

"My left is not my strongest side, but I can hold a sword."

Odin wasn't pleased. "Not good. Gentlemen, I am glad I called this meeting. At present my army is a one-handed swordsman and a pillock with an antler. My son is trying to stop Ragnarok in the hamr of a woman. And my eyes and ears have disappeared."

"No they haven't," said Freyr.

Odin paused, assessing him, as if to gauge the depth of his stupidity. "The ravens, who are my eyes and ears, have fallen to trickery. I believe it is imperative that we regain your sword. I cannot over emphasise this. Thor may buy us time. If he fails to find the dog, then my friend, yours may be a very short marriage."

Thora and Snorri were in the back streets of downtown Oslo, looking for the dog. Snorri's appearance had changed. He now resembled a tax accountant in his mid 60s. Thora was pleased with the practicality of the result. "It must be novel to walk around during the day," she said, in what was a rhetorical question.

"Yeah," said Snorri, "don't worry I'm delighted, but I feel that the appearance thing was perhaps a missed opportunity. Granted it's an improvement, but could your magical friend have picked Morten Harket?"

"You have been given a hamr which will pass unnoticed. It is perfect."

"I'm just saying, if we find ourselves in this situation again, I'll make a request."

"Find the dog and if all goes well I'll put in a word. There are gods so handsome that it makes the mortal eye bleed to look at them. Such will be your hamr. The Harket you speak of would be like an old bloodhound besides you."

"Some of my friends are old bloodhounds," countered a somewhat indignant Snorri.

"Should – when - you complete your task Odin may well look upon you favourably. As will everybody else. Consider this hamr a down payment. Either way your appearance will not change your fate. Only the norns can do that."

Snorri's ears pricked up, as much as a tax accountant's could. "What are they?"

"Have you not heard of the norns?"

"No. Are they a variety act?"

Thora indulged him with an explanation. "They visit you at the time of your birth and decide your life; there are other norns but the big three are Fate, Becoming and Obligation."

"Do these norns have mood swings? I'm not convinced they were on great form when I came into the world."

"There are good norns and bad norns, depends on the moment of your birth and who's on call. They work a shift system and it's a lottery."

Snorri hadn't had the best of luck. Clearly his father's amorous choices had a great deal to do with it. As an outcast who had seen his fair share of derision, it galled him that perhaps some magical entity was partially responsible. "It certainly does seem to be the case," he said.

"Obligation, the ability to resist temptation and to do that which you should, is key in most lives. I suspect that you have given to impulse and the lure to have your belly scratched rather than devote energy to your obligations."

"I have an obligation to myself to have my tummy scratched."

"Yet," concluded Thora, with a validatory flourish, "it's through meeting or avoiding our broader obligations that we come to be defined."

Snorri saw the point but it was not the first moral polemic he'd heard that he felt was directed at him. Besides he wasn't so bad. In an age of moral equivalence at least he stuck by his principles. "I would not kennel a dog to go on a date," he said.

Thora had a slight smile on her lips. "Perhaps you'd cancel a date to go to a kennel?"

"Now, I'm not like that. Anyhow, look at you, you're not exactly incognito. You look like a Vikings geek at Comic Con."

Thora looked herself up and down, taking in her appearance. "Is that a place where people fit in?"

"It's a place where the people who don't fit in like to go. Let's get you to a clothes shop, buy you a dress or something."

"I can't say I approve." She saw a shop called Thor Play, a fetish shop with mannequins in the window. "Although this looks alright. It's got my name on it."

"Ah, maybe not a great idea."

Thora didn't share Snorri's concern and strode towards the door. Inside, a slight gentleman in a latex vest looked up from behind the counter. He was Magnus, the proprietor. "Hallo darlings, can I help you?"

"I am looking to fit in," said Thora.

"Well, you've come to the right place. Everyone fits in, just be yourself. Isn't that right Clive?" Clive stood up from beneath the counter. He was wearing a furry costume and a muzzle. Snorri's eyes widened.

"Absolutely. Feel free," said Clive, slightly muffled. "There are no expectations here."

Thora took in his outfit, with the furry ears and animatronic wagging tail. "You haven't seen a dog called Bragi by any chance?"

Clive tipped his head to one side as he thought. "About 6ft tall, clipped moustache, Prince Albert?"

"Not that I'm aware of."

"We'll keep an eye open," said Magnus. "Always good to have new friends for Clive. So, what sort of thing were you looking for?"

Thora glanced around at a cornucopia of contraptions and costumery. "Something kind of Thor, but not obviously so. Subtle would be good."

"The Thor section's round the back, Clive will show you. We've just got a new range in rubber, hard wearing and I'm sure you'll have a lot of fun." He looked at Thora and Snorri with a wink.

Snorri blurted, "No, it's not... we're not..."

Magnus had heard it all before. "Whatever. Its 15% discount for new customers. So, daytime or evening wear?"

Thora was suitably impressed and felt vindicated by her choice of store. Clive scampered into the back room and they followed.


There was a booming knock on the front door in the dwarves chamber. It halted conversation and the dwarves became edgy, like listening rabbits in a burrow. Fjolmir got up to investigate. "I hope that's good news. Probably just the postman." After a minute he came back, ashen faced.

"Well," said Gandalf. "who is it? Anyone we know?"

"It's er... Odin."

There was an audible gasp and mutter from the trolls. Durin glowed at Fjolmir, "Well what have you done with him, did you let Odin in?"

"Odin in? No, he's waiting outside. He's Odin out."

"Is he Odin out for a hero?" asked Terry. Given the quality of his day so far, mythical beings had become commonplace, although he noted the tension in the room.

"He wants to have a word. With you."

The dwarves were not used to having Odin on their doorstep and Durin gave Terry a particularly hard stare. "Anything else you'd like to tell us?"

"Guilty of losing a dog. That's it. How bad can it be?"

Gandalf started at him "You are talking about the ruler of Heaven and Earth, and a very warlike individual. This guy makes Zeus look like a pussy cat."

Durin continued. "If he wants to he can make life difficult for you. We don't want him in here. I suggest you don't keep him waiting."

"It's a missing animal. Surely he wouldn't be unreasonable?"

Fjolmir was staggered at Terry's naivety. "He bloody well would. Follow me."

Terry followed as advised and was pushed rather abruptly through the secret door and into the statue park. Waiting for him was Odin.

"I thought it was time we met. You're the one who lost the dog? Terry, is it?"

After the big build up Terry was quite cautious, "Yes," he replied.

"Call me Odin. I have many names; Odin the All Father, Odin the Ass Kicker."

"Really?"

"No not really. Don't believe all that you hear. Let's speak plainly. Come, sit." Odin led and they sat on a nearby bench. Odin was relaxed. Terry rather awkward.

"How can I help?" asked Terry.

"Anything you'd like to talk about?"

"The dog perhaps?"

"Now," said Odin, "that's a good start. This dog of yours has risen significantly in his importance to the universe, as he is carrying a parasite. You could say quite a nasty, very big parasite. And you left him in a kennel whilst you pursued your lustful ends with a trapeze artist?"

Terry had a sense of being in front of a headmaster at school, a seemingly benign one, but still one with an unfathomable capacity for downside should the conversation go wrong. "This is unfortunately the case," he replied.

"Candour is good. You weren't to know the consequences. Allow me to explain. If things continue as they are, I will soon be fighting a giant wolf and there's no guarantee I'll win. In fact, according to prophecy, there's a good chance I'll be swallowed. As in swallowed alive by a giant wolf who is my nephew. So, I'm not in a hurry for this battle to commence."

"But aren't you the king of the Gods?"

"I am that indeed," he said proudly. Then his voice lowered, "but even the best kings are subject to time. I have been burning the candle at both ends for a while now. Do you know what I mean?"

Terry looked blank. He clearly didn't know what he meant.

"I battle a lot. I wage war in great cataclysmic conflicts. A lot. That's one end of the candle. Then there are the Valkyries. You've never seen a Valkyrie?"

Terry shrugged uneasily. "I know a Val Currie. As in Valerie Currie. She's a risk manager."

"Different," said Odin. "You wouldn't go charging halfway across Europe for a trapeze artist if you had. The fairest women in all the nine worlds, with a warrior's appetite. You know what I mean? Appetite for courtship lad."

"Ah," said Terry.

"So, at one end of the candle there's battle, and the other end there's courtship. What do you think's going to happen to the wick?" Odin stared at Terry, thoughtful. "Ultimately there's a limit. Man or God you can't go on forever, nor would you really want to. A stout, strong, waxy candle and a steady blaze is what you wish for. That being said, Fenir can go screw himself."

Odin's voice rose as he hit his stride. "My army at present is about as organised as a pack of clowns. Postponing Ragnarok would be an advantage. Apocalypse is not, especially, in anyone's best interest."

His hand clasped Terry's shoulder earnestly. "You need to rise up son and get on with saving the dog. Keep focused, put the circus women to one side and get the job done. You'll get your reward, and it'll make Valerie Currie look like a fish wife."

Terry's initial caution was fading and he found himself inspired by this curious figure. "I understand why they call you All Father. That was quite a pep talk."

"They call me that as I went through a purple patch a while back. We may be related." Odin faced Terry, staring with a blistering intensity. "Now, I suggest you get on with it. Search the city. The dwarves will help. There is considerable upside to you finding the dog, but mark my words Terry, you don't want to screw this up. I'll be on you like a bag of hammers."

Thora and Snorri left the shop. Thora was wearing a rubber outfit with lightning flashes and a leather jacket with 'Hammer Time' on the back. Snorri carried a large black carrier bag which was full to bursting. Thora zipped the jacket and stretched her arms back. "It is comfortable if not exactly practical, I approve."

"At least you're slightly less conspicuous. The jacket certainly works."

"Do you think so?" she asked with a slight turn. There was something about Thora which deterred Snorri from issuing too many compliments, and he felt it wise not to comment further. She was a curious lady with a small hammer and a penchant towards Thor costumes. Then again, he hadn't been on too many shopping expeditions, and normal is a very relative term anyway.

They turned down a side street and heard music from a bar with darkened windows. Thora put her nose against the glass to look through. It was indeed a shady establishment and her eyes were drawn to two ravens partying in the VIP section towards the back of the club.

"See those ravens," she said. "I know them. See how they cavort. Their good norns were having an off day. Their fate will make Ragnarok look like a summer holiday."

"I think I've just got the scent. Seems to be mixed with... perfume? Let's go."

Thora wasn't listening, she was lost in annoyance. "Despicable. By Hel's bed curtains, I'll knock their carcasses to Breidablik and back. Look at those dirty ravens."

Snorri tried to lead her away from the window. "Let's go Thora."

"The dog can wait. I'm going to have a word."

Snorri was especially reticent. "Really, I wouldn't go in there."

Thora opened the door of The Dirty Bird and stood there taking it in. It was a rough collection of low life's, pimps, drunks and gangsters. There were also various birds around, a pelican was walking across the room and a couple of parrots stood on the bar drinking stout from half pint glasses.

Thora was flabbergasted. "What is this place?"

"It's like a badly run aviary with beer. Not a place for the casual tourist. This is the most exotic hangout of the Oslo underworld. People only come here to make bad business or for millet. Or for both." Thora's appearance has caused interest in the bar, and a Nordic looking pimp strolled across.

"Hey honey pie, looking good, welcome to Dirty's. Ditch your Dad and come drink with Big Erik."

"I'm here to see the birds," said Thora. "Stand out of my way."

"Oh, you like the birds?" said Erik. "You in luck girl, just wait till you meet Inger. We share everything." He called towards the bar. "Inger get your hot little bootie over here."

A tall pretty girl in a hand knitted jumper came across and draped herself on Erik's shoulder. "She's cute. Hi lovely, I'm Inger from Kongsvinger."

"She's the biggest svinger in town," claimed Erik. "Come have a drink."

Erik took Thora's elbow to lead her, and Snorri winced in anticipation. In one fluid movement, Thora grabbed Erik and threw him over the bar. The other drinkers were used to fights at Dirty's and barely noticed. Thora moved towards the ravens, brushing past Inger, Snorri moved in close for a moment.

"Sorry for my friend," he said. "I could give you my number?"

Inger sniffed the air. "You smell of dog food."

Snorri felt that on balance this wasn't meant as a plus. "Fine. Maybe later then."

A large gangster stepped in front of Thora. He was a foot taller, built and dressed in dark flashy clothes. He gestured to the ravens. "I'm sorry lady but they're busy."

"I know them," said Thora. "They're not too busy to see me."

The man stood his ground. "I can guarantee they are. You handled Erik but if you play with me you'll get burned."

His eyes flicked with flames, and Thora noticed his jacket start to steam with heat.

"Surt?" she said. "What are you doing here?"

Surt took in her outfit and appearance. "Do I know you?"

Thora twirled and caught her hammer on its strap a couple of times, like a trick shooting gunslinger. A look of recognition passed over Surt. "Nice hamr."

"You too," said Thora. "Step aside."

"The ravens are the least of your worries."

"The ravens are not your concern," replied Thora.

"They're here for their pleasure. And as bait. We thought you might show up, but really, as a maiden? This is a surprise... daughter of Odin." A few of the other pub thugs snigger. "Or maybe we shouldn't be so shocked? God of Thunder... thighs."

Thora winced and tightened her grip on Mjollnir. "Enjoy mocking me whilst you can. Soon you will be a corpse. And that's a dead Surt." She looked around but nobody appeared to appreciate the taunt. Around the pub a dozen men bristled. Ready to fight. "Are there any other fire giants here?" she asked.

The men slowly put their hands up. One of them brought Surt a Viking style belt. "Do you know this, Thor?" asked Surt. "It is Megingard, your girdle of strength."

"It's not a girdle, it's a belt," she clarified.

"Given your current hamr I think it's more appropriate to call it a girdle."

"It could be a truss," interjected Snorri. "Like a surgical support?"

"It is a belt," said Thora, definitively. "How did you get it?"

Surt indicated towards the ravens. Hugin cleared his throat. "Do you have any idea how many ravens it takes to carry a girdle all the way from Asgard?"

Thora's eyes narrowed as she glowered at the birds. "You devils."

"Two," continued Hugin. "Only two highly motivated birds. Who are finally getting a kick at the ball."

Surt examined the girdle thoughtfully. "Of course, a girdle of strength worn inside out would leave you as weak as a kitten."

"No it wouldn't."

"Yes it would," said Surt. "We've tested it. Are you getting in the girdle or do we have to put you in it?"

Thora glanced at Snorri who by now was stood by her side. "This could get messy. It is not your fight. Leave whilst you can."

"Twelve against one?" he replied. "Nah. That's not right. I'll have a piece of that."

"They're not men. They are fire giants." She could see Snorri was getting geed up.

"No, that's alright. I'd like some." He set his feet like a boxer and raised his voice, talking to Surt. "Bring it on. I'll have some of that."

Near a window, a parrot and a budgerigar were perched on a stand, overlooking the confrontation. The parrot whispered, "This is going to kick off. Go get the Dwarves."

The budgerigar fidgeted but did nothing. Surt looked Snorri up and down then spoke to Thora, laden with sarcasm. "Who's that? Your pet?"

"I'm Snorri Snakker. Part Troll, part golden retriever. All bad."

"Are you going to put a leash on that or am I?"

Snorri stepped forward and pushed Surt in the chest. He was surprised and knocked back a couple of steps. He angered and rushed at Snorri. Snorri sidestepped and Surt pushed Thora. Thora's feet were braced but still slid back halfway across the pub, knocking tables and chairs. Thora looked serious, took a stance and started twirling her hammer.

The parrot spoke aside to the budgerigar out the corner of his beak. "It's on. Hurry."

The budgerigar flew out of the upper window, a porthole used by visiting members of the avian community, leaving The Dirty Bird and the starting fight behind. It flew at street level, a blur of concerted motion all the way to Frogner Park where it found the right statue and knocked its beak against its navel. "Come on come on." it twittered, like a getaway driver waiting on a heist.

It knocked the door a bit more frantically. The door swung open. Gandalf hadn't known who to expect, there had been a glut of visitors recently and the secret door was becoming something of a thoroughfare. Still, he looked surprised.

"What on Earth do you want? A bloody busy day this is turning out to be."

The bird landed on his finger. "Fight breaking out at Dirty's," it gasped, between tiny lungfuls of breath. "The parrot says bring Dwarves".

"Dwarves? Well, I'm afraid I can't help you there. There's only me here. Fjolmir and Durin are out on a search party."

The budgerigar looked impatiently at him. "One dwarf will have to do."

A rough voice pitched in from behind him. "One dwarf and a small troop of battle ready trolls," said Rocky. "He's not alone. Who's fighting?"

The budgerigar took a deep breath. "They're in disguise," it said, "An undercover god, looks like it's Thor, and a sleaze ball who could be Surt. And an undistinguished man who says he's a golden retriever."

Rocky was resolute. "Thora and Snorri. They need help? Then off to battle we go!"

Gandalf turned to address the passageway. "Hang on, hang on. Thor? The dwarf kicker? He's no friend. And Snorri, that wet nosed drittsekk? Screw them. Let's sit this one out."

"No," said Rocky, "they're good guys." He considered this further. "Snorri, ok granted that's fair, but they're helping Terry in his quest."

"He's a rompehull as well," said Gandalf.

The budgerigar, still perched on Gandalf's finger despite his gesticulations, steadied himself and interrupted. "I think it's a trap, they were expecting Thor."

"I've heard enough," said Rocky. "Lead the way."

"Oh, for goodness sake..." said Gandalf. He went into the main room and came out carrying his axe. "This better not take long."

Inside a very modern minimalist observatory, designed with impeccable taste, Heimdall, a tall albino in couture, was meeting with Freyr. "Can you just have another look?" he asked Heimdall. "Odin says it's important."

"Would it not have been easier not to have lost your invincible sword? Especially on the eve of Ragnarok?" Heimdall clearly wasn't going to make this easy.

"I didn't lose it, I gave it away," admitted Freyr.

"I have seen a lot, in many worlds in many realms, over many years. But that is possibly the dumbest thing I'm aware of."

"Don't judge until you've been in love," said Freyr. He looked around, taking in the decor. "This place is unusual, not especially Asgardian... and neither are you."

"I've watched the world for a long time. I've seen a lot of things; war, peace, the modern age... fashion. You can't be an observer for as long as I have and not develop some style." Heimdall was quietly pleased that Freyr had noticed. "Oh, you mean my skin? I was born of nine mothers, all albino. I am called the whitest of the white."

"I hadn't heard that."

Heimdall shrugged. "Some people call me this. I suppose people say all sorts."

"I see. Do you mind me asking? Bifrost... the rainbow bridge. Was this your idea?"

"Nine mothers," emphasised Heimdall. "Three of them obsessed with unicorns. It was hardly going to be constructed from pre-stressed concrete."

"Very nice it is too," said Freyr, "and the flames are not overstated. Now about my sword. Would it be too much to take another sweep?"

Heimdall looked irritated, albeit briefly. "Oh ok, just for you because you've been so kind about the bridge. Not everybody appreciates design. But one look that's all."

Heimdall put his eye to the telescope. It moved at great speed, a blur scanning all the realms. "Found it," he said. "Is the man who took it thin with glasses."

"That's him."

"But he's with a squirrel. Is that Ratatosk?"

Freyr took the telescope from Heimdall. "Let me have a look at that." He saw a man showing off a sword in front of a squirrel. The man was laughing and bragging, swinging the sword around.

"Looks like your opportunist friend has been working with a squirrel," commented Heimdall.

"What kind of man deals with Ratatosk?"

"Not a man of great moral fibre. You probably know that already. Seems that someone wants that sword out of play. And here's a clue, I would imagine that someone hides nuts for the winter."

"Thanks Heimdall."

Heimdall extended his hand. "Snowdrop please. You're a friend now."

"Snowdrop..." Freyr was uneasy with the term but continued, "can you not use this thing to find the dog? Has Odin not spoken with you?"

"He has. There appears to be some kind of mystical cloud around Oslo which is obscuring my sight. Or it could be just cloudy."

"Is there much cloud elsewhere?"

"No, it's clear," said Heimdall. Whereas he didn't have a strong interest in weather, he took pride in attention to detail. "Quite sunny around all southern Norway."

Freyr considered all this thoughtfully. "Sounds like pockets of cloud," he said, "but these are not normal times. Set the bridge to drop me near Ratatosk. I think it's about time I had a word."

An aggravated dwarf with an axe was running through the streets. Pedestrians jumped out of the way; some people videoed on their phones. He burst through the door of the Dirty Bird. Thora was being restrained by Surt and Snorri was held by several thugs. Thora was wearing the belt.

"There you are." Gandalf pointed his axe in the vicinity of the group. "Release them."

"Who the hell are you little man?" said Surt.

"Little?" Gandalf fumed. "I'll have you know I'm average height for my kin." Gandalf barreled his way towards Surt, and the thugs menaced towards him. Before they could reach Gandalf the men were punched and thrown by the invisible trolls. "Have that... Come on..."

Gandalf looked around. There were no thugs left to punch, the scene was of dispossessed henchmen lying around in various states of injury and unconsciousness. Snorri unbuckled Thora's belt, turned it the right way round and wore it himself. He squared up to Surt and floored him in a single blow. "You're toast pal," he said, standing over him.

Gandalf came over to the fallen Surt and started putting the boot in. "Who's the big man now?"

Thora moved Gandalf off him. "He's had enough, easy. There's business to attend to and we've been held up here." Thora walked over to the ravens.

"Hey," said Hugin, "no let's not be hasty." Thora swung a punch and connected with both. They both spun in looping circles around their perch.

"Possibly excessive," remarked Snorri. He sniffed the air. "I've still got the scent but it's faint. I hope it's not too late."


Freyr stood behind a tree in a rural Asgardian pasture, listening to the imbecilic chatter beyond, He stepped into view, taking Skirnir by surprise. Ratatosk shot straight up the tree as soon as he saw him.

"I've found you Skirnir. You know what I want."

"I have a good idea," said Skirnir, recovering himself slightly. "But it was freely given, if by a fool."

"The name calling isn't helpful," replied Freyr. "If the sword is returned freely I will let you live."

A voice came down from the tree. Ratatosk was hidden in the thick foliage. "It is yours Skirnir, it was traded as part of a legally binding verbal contract for a service which was performed to all parties satisfaction. Don't give it to him."

Freyr had not encountered Ratatosk before, but he was as bothersome as his reputation suggested. "You are very brave talking from up there." He cast Skirnir a wry glare. "Tell me that you're not taking orders from a squirrel?"

"He is of his own free mind," came the voice from the tree.

"I am indeed," Skirnir agreed. "But it is also wise to listen to good counsel."

Freyr grew exasperated. "Skirnir, you have been played by this bushy tailed trickster."

"Oh," Skirnir replied, his tone turned to mockery, "I think that it's you who has been played. It was Ratatosk's idea to set you up with Gerd. But are you not happy? And all for the price of a simple sword."

"Set up? No, that's not true."

A couple of leaves fell as Ratatosk hopped about. "It may or may not have an element of truth, and if it did you should be grateful. Yet I am an innocent party."

"You are the squirrel of deceit," accused Freyr. "I need this sword for Ragnarok. Who are you working for, are you Loki's puppet?"

"I am not working for anyone," came the voice, "but if I was, they'd be working for me."

Freyr turned to Skirnir. "How do you put up with him? Give me your sword and I will absolve you of your crime."

"What crime?" objected Ratatosk, interrupting like a legal counsel. "There isn't one."

"Your crime," continued Freyr, "of being an accomplice to this squirrel. Of deceit, of treachery, of plotting the downfall of Asgard at Ragnarok. I will ask once again for my sword."

"You're not having it," said Skirnir. "Unless of course you can take it."

Freyr raised his antler in anger and circled Skirnir. He attacked in a series of strokes which Skirnir parried easily. Freyr thrust and Skirnir struck the antler breaking it in half. "Now you have half an antler. Yield?"

"It is indeed a mighty sword. But you will give me it, in exchange for the squirrel's life. I didn't want to do this, but it's your choice. The sword or the squirrel."

Skirnir leant on his sword and considered the demand. "I don't like to point this out but surely it's wise to take a hostage before issuing demands? Even if you did have the squirrel I'm not giving up my sword."

"We'll see about that." Freyr leapt to a low hanging branch and pulled himself up into the dense foliage. The noise of an excited scampering and a man clambering filled the rural silence. Skirnir watched as the tree gently shook.


In a back alley on Oslo's east side, Bragi was sniffing along the road, watched by a gang of dogs. They approached him with attitude.

"Hey meatball, you're on the wrong side of town," said a Lundehund in a slightly torn quilted jumper.

"This is our patch," said an Elkhound with a studded collar. "Are you a tourist? I hope you got medical insurance. What you got for us Buttercup?"

"Come on," said the Lundehund, "let's have a sniff." They stalked him, approaching with noses twitching.

Bragi looked at them - his eyes glowed red, and he spoke with a lisp like a snake. "Go sniff yourselves, you little runts"

The dogs turned tail and scattered, yelping. A seductive voice came from further down the alley. It was the Afghan draped on top of a parked Harley Davidson.

"Hey bad dog," purred the Afghan, "why the dirty mouth?"

Bragi looked up and saw the Afghan outside a biker bar, appearing like a vision. The door to the bar was ajar and 'Now I wanna be your dog' started to spill out from a jukebox.

"You're clearly the leader of the pack," the Afghan continued. "You bring out the pooch in me. Woof."

"Beat it Bjollok, I'm busy. I'm looking for a horned god to join in battle."

The Afghan feigned shock. "Aren't we all darling. Don't you think that appearances can be deceptive though? I mean, here we are; you a cute little fluffy terrier and me this elegant Afghan in a luxuriant coat."

The Afghan's voice became more serpentine and seductive. "But your voice, so sexy. If I didn't know better I'd say you had the spirit of a serpent inside you."

"So apt of you to say so." He sniffed the Afghan's coat. "Familiar scent, but I can't think from where?"

"Spent a long time going round the world, chasing your tail?"

They circled each other. "Who are you?" asked Bragi.

"That doesn't matter, let's just say I like your spirit - your serpent side inside you. Maybe we should date?"

Bragi flattened his ears. "That's starting to sound splendid."

Durin ran round the corner with Terry. "Bragi, get away from that dirty pup. It's me, Terry. Don't you remember?" Bragi's eyes cleared and his tail wagged as he walked a few steps towards Terry. Then undecided he looked between Terry and the Afghan. "Look boy," Terry continued, "I've got a sausage. You like sausages."

The Afghan adopted a coquettish pose. "Never mind the sausage, get a load of me."

Bragi weighed up the options, given a choice between romance with a mysterious stranger or Terry with sausages, he knew what to do, besides if the Afghan would understand if she was really his friend. Bragi walked to Terry with his tail wagging. Terry threw him the sausage and he happily devoured it.

Just then, Thora and Snorri burst round the corner. Snorri saw the Afghan, and Bragi and Thora faced off. Despite their changed appearances, the two old foes instantly recognised each other.

Snorri and the Afghan eyed each other. Snorri flirted, barking smoothly in Terrier. The Afghan was unimpressed. "Hiss off Snorri," she replied, and turned to watch the standoff.

Thora and Bragi cautiously advanced on each other. The dog's eyes turned red and his tail started spinning. He levitated slowly to a certain height then fired a flame ball, from an obtuse angle, towards Thora. Thora dived out the way. "Take cover!"

Terry, Snorri and Durin took cover - diving behind bins. Durin advanced with a bin lid as a shield. "I am Durin Oakenshield and I hide from no-one."

Bragi fired at his shield and knocked him over. He fired at Thora who blocked with the rock hammer - deflecting the fire ball at the Afghan which singed her tail. She ran in circles then rolled on the ground to put the fire out.

Thora tried jumping up at Bragi and swinging the hammer - Bragi kept flying out of reach. Durin shouted, "Exorcise him, exorcise the dog. It's the only way."

"I think he's had quite enough exercise," remarked Terry, hiding behind a bin. "Have you a better idea?"

"No, exorcise as in exorcism. Use the sausage."

Terry held what was left of the sausage. "He's eaten half of it," he said.

"I've got two left," shouted Durin. "Make a cross laddie."

Terry looked over the bin. "Are you mad?!"

Durin threw the sausages. Terry put them together and made a cross then emerged from his hiding place fearing the worst. Bragi's head was spinning round but stopped - he backed away from the cross.

Terry spoke with an authority he didn't know he could muster. "In the name of all that is Holy, release this dog." Bragi darted around in the air a little, like an angry hornet.

"You're my favourite dog," said Terry, still holding up the cross. "Good boy. I was wrong to put you in a kennel and I'll never do it again. Foul serpent, I command you to go back to the fjord from which you came. You have no place here. Release him now!"

The dog flatulated, hovered for a moment - then fell from the sky. Terry dropped the sausages and, in a slow motion moment, ran to catch him. The dog was motionless for a while, and they thought they'd lost him. Then, he came round with a little bark and licked Terry's face.

Durin put the fetters on the Afghan. "Come blood uncle," said Thora. "You go to see Odin to explain yourself then back to your cave. Your wife is waiting."

The Afghan whimpered a little, looking guilty and sad. Thora noticed Megingard still round Snorri's waist. "I see you still have my belt," she said.

"Ah, about that. You know, someone's got to clean up the mean streets of Oslo. I think I'm cut out for vigilante work. I may not be the champion that Oslo needs, but I'm the only one they've got."

"I like the way you handled Surt. Let's say that it's still my belt but I'll let you borrow it for a while."

"And the appearance thing? This one's great but if Odin was to insist..."

"I'll have a word," said Thora. "It's still my belt though."

"Yeah... Right."

Terry was still holding Bragi. "Come on boy, it's time to go home."

Bragi answered in quite a sophisticated voice. "I quite agree. I'm absolutely pooped."

Terry looked astonished and Thora stepped forward, not sure whether to engage. Bragi saw her approach and continued in a hurry, "I'm fine totally good, not possessed at all."

"But how is this possible?" remarked a visibly shocked Terry.

"When the serpent left I just felt different, stronger in some way, and obviously speaking is an unforeseen bonus."

"You could say that," said Terry. "Let's go home, you can tell me all about it."

They all laughed and started to walk off but stopped. Now the battle was over they noticed a certain police presence in the area. They were surrounded by police cars and marksmen with rifles.

They all slowly raised their hands and looked at Bragi, who sat up straight and innocently raised his paws.


In a Norwegian family home on Christmas morning, a little girl was excited to receive a dog basket. She lifted out an adorable Afghan puppy. Overwhelmed with delight she embraced the dog, who wagged its tail and looked over her shoulder.

As she hugged him there was a barely audible hiss. Nobody noticed, but the dog's eyes turned bloodshot red.

# About the author

David is a screenwriter, author and actor. He graduated in Physics with Marketing from Lancaster University, gained a Masters in International Business from Manchester Business School. He is a Teessider by birth and a Yorkshireman for ceremonial purposes.

Other works by David A. Burt

Rage Against The Cuisine

This is a largely fictional cookbook full of exciting and workable recipes.

'One of the most entertaining reads I've had, a clever look at the culinary absurdity of modern food culture combining this with recipes, wit and an analytical look at why we eat certain foods. If you're looking for a Kindle book to entertain and wile away those hours getting to work on public transport, this is it! Rage Against the Cuisine is highly recommended!'

Rage Against The Cuisine is available through Amazon and www.rageagainstthecuisine.com

Printed in Great Britain
by Amazon